D1824523

THE FROLIK DEFECTION

THE
FROLIK
DEFECTION

by

JOSEF FROLIK

LEO COOPER · LONDON

First Published in Great Britain 1975 by
LEO COOPER LTD.
196 Shaftesbury Avenue, London WC2H 8JL

Copyright © 1975 by Josef Frolik

ISBN 0 85052 179 3

Printed in Great Britain by
Clarke, Doble and Brendon Ltd.
at Plymouth

'*Those who were caught by the great illusion of our time, and have lived through its intellectual and moral debauch, either give themselves up to a new addiction of the opposite type or are condemned to pay with a lifelong hangover.*'

Arthur Koestler: *The God That Failed*

Contents

v

This book was written by the author in English. At his request the publishers then recast it in a more conventional style. The final draft was then approved by the author. The publishers would like to thank Mr Josef Josten and Mr Michael Tregenza for their help in elucidating some of the mysteries of the Czech political scene. They are also grateful to the following for permission to reproduce photographs in this book: Camera Press Ltd, the Keystone Press Agency, Free Czech Information, Mr K. Fields, Michael Cummings/Beaverbrook Newspapers, the *Daily Mail*, London and *The Times*.

Foreword

I am a defector. My dictionary defines the act of defecting as 'abandoning a person or a cause; apostasy; revolt; backsliding'. Not to put too fine an edge on it, I am a *traitor*, who fled his native country, bearing with him important secrets, which could only injure that country's security and intelligence services. Indeed, when I arrived in Washington four years ago, CIA Director Helms shook my hand and exclaimed enthusiastically, 'Joe, you have brought the Czech (Intelligence) Service down on its knees!' But, believe me, I was not proud to hear those enthusiastic words of congratulation. For in my soul I am a loyal Czech who saw no other way of revealing the true character of the régime which presently rules my country than by defecting. If you like, I voted with my feet against communism. And to do so, I lost virtually everything I valued and held dear: my mother, my homeland, my friends and my position. Today I am just an exile, whose life is permanently threatened—my old service will never forgive my 'treachery'—and who can never 'come in from the cold'.

For seventeen years I was a member of Czech Intelligence, at home in Prague, in London and in foreign capitals all over the Middle East, until I took the step which made me one of the most senior Eastern Intelligence men to 'go West' since the War. In those years I lived in a State which is just one huge concentration camp, a human cage encircled by barbed wire, guarded against escape by minefields and machine-guns, and watched over by an all-powerful secret police. It was (and is) a State where everything is secret, false and prohibited (unless expressly authorized) and where one sleeps with one eye open, always waiting for that ominous 4 o'clock-in-the-morning ring at the door-bell which indicates the arrival of the secret police.

It was (and is) a State which has been converted from the one-time 'America of Europe' to one where one cannot obtain razor blades which are sharp, refrigerators that cool, automobiles safe to run; where scores of official lackeys must give their consent before your child can attend a high school or you may go off on a week's vacation.

It was (and is) a State run by bloodthirsty monsters, who once carried out the Gestapo's dirty work and now do the same for the Russian KGB, perverse little sadists who enjoy wielding the whip of power or degenerate profligates who spend the nation's hard-earned money as fast as any of the West's 'jet-set'.

And it was (and is) a State which ran an aggressive intelligence war against the West, spending fortunes to pervert, corrupt and blackmail those Westerners who could give them the Intelligence they want. Then, as now, the officers of Czech Intelligence believed that 'the world is marching towards communism. No enemy can stop us,' to use Khrushchev's words of 1959. In every country and in every class—German generals, French counter-espionage officers, British trade unionists, Middle Eastern politicos, American gangsters—they found (and find) their dupes, who will supply them with the information which they hope will enable the East 'to bury you', as Khrushchev, too, once promised Communism would do with the West.

This, then, is my story of the years leading up to my defection and what occurred in the soul of one Czech Intelligence man and changed him from an enthusiastic communist to someone who hated the system like poison so that, in the end, he had only one aim—to collect all the secret data about the personalities, aims and espionage activities of the Czech régime he could, in order one day to reveal it, in all its bitter perversion, to the Free World. By doing that, I felt I might in some small way repay my debt to my unfortunate country.

JOSEF FROLIK

November, 1974
Somewhere in the USA

Prologue

'The soul of the spy is somehow the model of us all.'

Jacques Barzun

It was now midday. From where I had stopped my little, over-laden Skoda in the last village before the border, I could see the striped barrier, the barbed wire, the watch-towers and, more frighteningly, the border guards lounging around in the June sunshine.

I turned to my wife. She was white-faced and still very nervous after last night's near escape, when a tourist bus parked outside the hotel where we had stayed had been thoroughly burgled. She knew as well as I did that if that had happened to our little Skoda it would have meant death for us both, perhaps even for our son sitting, unusually quiet, in the back.

'I think it's time now to fill in the cards,' I said quietly, trying to keep my voice under control. I handed her some coloured post-cards which contrasted oddly with our own mood of near despair at that moment. She chose one to send to her father, who was dying of cancer in a Prague clinic. With hands that trembled slightly she began to write the message that we had decided on when we planned our escape. I started to write cards to my mother and two sisters: 'Holiday greetings . . . weather wonderful . . . see you in a month's time. Your Josef.'

In one month's time, if my plans worked out, I would be seven thousand kilometres away and almost certainly I would never see my family again. If my plans didn't work out, the likeliest place in which my family and I could expect to be reunited was the death cell!

We finished the cards and I looked at my wife. Her eyes were full of the unspoken question, 'Can't we still go back, for my father's sake and for the child?' I shook my head and pressed her hand gently. There was no going back. It would be only a matter of days now before my former colleagues in Czech Intelligence

1

would be making that well-known early morning call at my apartment to haul me off to God knows what grisly fate.

Since the Russian occupation of my country, those Czechs who had sided with the occupiers had rapidly become accustomed to the KGB's sadistic methods. In addition, I knew from my own sources that my dismissal from the service, which was to take effect from 1 August, 1969, would be announced on or around 30 June. Thereafter, for at least five years, I would be forbidden to cross any border. It had to be now or never.

I took the card from my wife, got out of the car, and put it and my own three into the letter-box. It would be our last contact with those we loved most. We would never see them again. I climbed back into the car and the little Skoda, loaded with top secret information which any Western Intelligence Service would have given a fortune to possess, was soon moving towards the frontier post.

The border guard held up a small metal disc on the end of a stick as a sign for us to stop. He was obviously bored, but he went through his routine as meticulously as was expected of him in these days when a large number of Czechs were trying to escape from the country. He looked at my visa. 'I see you are going to Bulgaria?' he said.

I nodded.

'Why don't you go to Yugoslavia?' he said, smiling. 'Better than Bulgaria any day.'

I breathed a sigh of relief. The guard was harmless; indeed his remark showed that he might even have helped a would-be escaper. Bulgaria was one of our new enemies, a country which had helped to occupy us, whereas Yugoslavia had remained neutral and was now the gateway to freedom for many escaping Czechs.

The guard raised his hand to wave us on to the bridge over the Danube, the border between the two countries, and I was about to drive off when a man in the uniform of the feared STB, the State Security Service, stepped out of the hut and held up his hand. 'Stop!' he ordered. I stopped. I had worked with the STB for seventeen years. I knew it didn't pay to disobey their orders.

'Get out.'

I got out, followed by my wife and son.

'Open the cases.'

Trying to control the trembling of my hands, I began to open them. With the callousness of his kind, he rummaged through the personal things which the first case contained. Nothing. He started on the second. Almost immediately he found the three cartons of American cigarettes which I had brought back with me from one of my spymaster trips to Africa the previous year, which had earned me—ironically enough—a medal from the Czech President himself.

'What are these?' he asked.

Was he smart enough to realize that the 600 American 'Camels' were an ideal bribe in Eastern Europe, starved of good tobacco? That was why I had brought them with me.

I said simply, 'They're the only brand I can smoke.'

He sniffed and continued to rummage in the cases. If he decided to give the car a really good going-over he would soon find the top secret documents which I had sealed underneath the chassis. But no; he grunted and said, 'All right; on your way.'

I started to repack the cases, while he watched us from the side of the road. I had just finished when he pointed to the dog-eared copy of the Czech classic *The Good Soldier Schweik* which was lying on the back window ledge. 'What's that?' he asked.

By now I had recovered my nerve. The discipline, based on years of active Intelligence work, had reasserted itself. 'Schweik,' I answered, holding up the book, which contained the cipher to the vital documents hidden under the car. 'It makes good holiday reading, doesn't it?'

'I suppose so,' he answered. I don't suppose the big oaf had read a book since he left primary school, save for the STB's bible—the official regulations.

A moment later I was rattling across the bridge over the Danube between Czechoslovakia and Hungary. I would never see my country again, but I didn't look back. I had a long and dangerous journey ahead of me and there was no time to waste on sentiment. The Frolik Defection had begun.

The Initiation (1952–1960)

'The game of espionage is too dirty for anyone but a gentleman.'
British Intelligence Officer

ONE

The Apprenticeship

I was born a bastard. My mother was a seamstress. My father I never knew. Later, when I was of primary school age, my mother married a widower with four children and moved to another village, leaving me to be reared by my grandfather, a miner who had retired from the mines with silicosis and a small pension.

My mother still continued to play a role in my life. My step-father, whose name I now bear, was a passionate communist and he soon convinced my mother to join the illegal Czech Communist Party. Thus when the Nazis came in 1939, my step-father was one of the first to be put in a concentration camp, joining my communist uncle—my idol—who had preceded him by a few days. My step-father did not survive. Rather than become a stoolpigeon and betray everything he had held sacred from his early youth, he threw himself on the electric wire at Mauthausen concentration camp near Linz, in Austria. My uncle was not so steadfast. One day I was to learn that the Party 'hero' had feet of clay, but that was a long way off.

In spite of the war, the shortages and the dangers of working in the Czech Resistance, I grew up to be a broad, strong boy, just short of six foot, enjoying all the usual boyish pleasures, while waiting for that blessed day when the Allies would come to free my oppressed people from the Nazi yoke.

Finally that triumphant, blossoming spring of 1945 arrived, full of Russian harmonica music, tanks with red stars painted on their turrets, and happy soldiers in dirty, earth-coloured tunics. It was a spring replete with tempting promises from the new 'liberators' from the east about a world without wars, without madness, without concentration camps, a spring in which I shared a belief common in my country that no other society could be as humane and decent as the one projected by my mother, my uncle and all the rest of the 'returnees' who had suffered at German hands for the communist cause.

How naïve I was! Little did I realize that at the very time when Rudenko, the Soviet prosecutor at Nuremberg, was accusing the Nazi war criminals of 'crimes against humanity', many thousands of innocent people were being transported from the newly 'liberated' countries to a different kind of concentration camp, which did not bear the cynical Nazi inscription, 'Work Makes Free' over its gate, but the five-pointed red star of Soviet Communism.

But in the immediate post-war world I was too busy starting a new life—preparing myself for a career in accountancy, which found its culmination as chief-of-administration on the communist paper *Rude Pravo* at the great age of 21.

In 1949 I was called up for my two years' military service. They were hell. Our officers and NCOs were mostly turncoats or hastily trained buffoons, spewing empty phrases about the new communist régime in Czechoslovakia and trying to turn us into shining defenders of Central Europe's most recent 'socialist' state. One of our officers, a fool named Kubaric, was so thick he didn't even know where Paris was! On one occasion he had the stupidity to pull out a battalion of recruits fighting a forest fire to send them on a routine firing exercise at the ranges. The result was one forest less in the new 'Workers' and Peasants' Republic'!

But I quickly learnt that one need not take that sort of thing lying down, especially if one came from a good communist background, as I did, and had no 'bourgeois' skeletons in the cupboard. Thus, at the end of my career, when I found out that the officers of the 2nd Infantry Regiment had stolen millions of crowns worth of jewels, paintings and tapestry from the famous monastery at Tepla, I mailed a report to the Third Directorate of Counter-Intelligence (Military) in Prague. The result was not exactly what I had expected. Almost by return of post I received a letter stating that the 'Party needed me'. What did it need an enthusiastic young accountant for? It needed him as a recruit for the Czech Secret Service!

I joined the Service on 1 December, 1952, with the rank of 1st Sergeant in the Finance Directorate of the new Ministry of

Security, and almost at once I got a taste of the kind of person I would be working with.

Staff Captain Jodas, an arrogant, dark-haired officer who was my chief, told me, 'Do you know, this very morning as I was coming to work a damned Army Colonel failed to salute me. I soon sorted him out. I stood him to attention for ten solid minutes to teach him a proper sense of respect for a member of the State Security Organization'. He stared at me sourly. 'I can see that you are an educated and conscientious man, Sergeant, who won't take the kind of nonsense that you had to stand in the Army. I can't blame you.' Then he dismissed me to my duties.

At first they were pretty routine, consisting basically of checking the Ministry's accounts. But in 1953 I was transferred to the newly set up Main Accounts Department, which began to give me some insight into the methods of the Security organization and the men who ran it. My new chief was an embittered Major, suffering from an ulcer, who hated the whole world and was only concerned with his pornographic pictures. But he was harmless in comparison with the men I now started to come into contact with in the course of my duty tours through the provinces.

There was Major Janousek, for example, an interrogator, renowned for his cruelty and his incredible stupidity, whose favourite means of obtaining information was to place a metal bucket over the suspect's head and beat on it with a stick until the man 'confessed'. An old chestnut was told of him that when an Egyptian mummy fell into his hands and was given the bucket treatment it confessed!

But even Janousek was harmless in comparison with the officers who ran the State's uranium mines, worked by at least 60,000 slave labourers. When these exhausted, broken men died, the camp personnel simply instituted 'strike raids' locally and large numbers of innocent men were rounded up and condemned to a living death in the slave camps.

Slowly my naive young eyes began to be opened. The 'former people', as potential enemies of the State were called, were everywhere. Ex-members of the scouts, Rotary Club, Salvation Army, YMCA, the churches, Anglo-American clubs—anyone with the remotest connection with the West or the pre-war Czech State infrastructure—was regarded as a possible spy and supervised by a whole host of counter-intelligence agents. Indeed, as the humorists in my department used to joke, 'One half of Czechoslovakia is spying on the other half!'

The Deputy Minister of the Interior, the man who really ran the whole *apparat* at that time, was Colonel Antonin Prchal, a small, red-haired man, still in his early thirties. His past was highly dubious. During the German Occupation he had been a pimp, running a stable of whores under cover of being a professional dancer at the German Officers' Club at the Lucerna Bar. But he had also been an agent of the notorious Prague Gestapo boss, Boehm. Surprisingly enough, when the war ended, nothing happened to him. Indeed, he soon rose to high rank within the Czech service. Today, knowing more about the methods of the KGB, I can guess why Beria[1] protected him against any accusation from the Czech side. The Russians had Prchal's wartime file and were blackmailing him. What better position to have a Russian agent in than at the top of another intelligence service!

Prchal usually came to work at ten, an hour later than Jodas. About noon he got down to reading the daily intelligence reports. But his 'socialist enthusiasm' did not last long. By two o'clock he was playing tennis on his private court. Around five he returned to the office to watch the screening of his favourite pre-war American horror films—Frankenstein, Dracula and the like—or pornographic films of 'suspects' filmed by the security service, in particular homosexual affairs.

But 'business' really started at eleven in the evening when he called in the heads of the various departments for their daily reports, after which he would give free rein to his perverted sense of humour at the expense of his subordinates. In a room behind his office he had had an extensive model railway laid out, complete with tunnels, bridges, stations, papier-mâché countryside and the like. This had apparently been built for the sole purpose of humiliating his underlings. Thus it was that generals, colonels and majors, grey-haired, dignified men with years of service to the State behind them, were forced to 'play trains' under Prchal's contemptuous gaze.

[1] Lavrenty Pavlovich Beria (1899–1953) was USSR Commissar for Internal Affairs 1938–45. After the war he organized the mass deportations from Eastern Europe. In the struggle for power after Stalin's death he was arrested and shot.

Some of the men involved could have been his father, as, for instance, 60-year-old General Karel Smisek, crawling around on his stiff knees, moving trains and stations while the 'sword of the working class' (as President Gottwald had once called Prchal) drank imported Scotch at the private bar. Often it was four o'clock in the morning before Prchal would allow his unwilling 'playmates' to leave for their homes.

A colleague of that time told me just how arrogant Prchal, that 'embodiment of the pure, selfless proletarian', could be. During the Slansky trials,[1] the Minister of Justice, Rais, repeatedly telephoned to ask if he could talk to Prchal. Time and again Prchal put him off. In the end Prchal got sick of the Minister of Justice's importuning. He told a subordinate, 'Tell the Comrade Minister he can go and kiss my ass!'

The subordinate dutifully repeated Prchal's message to Rais, then one of the most powerful men in the State, and what was the reaction? Rais stuttered, 'Yes, yes, Comrade, please excuse me. Honour to Labour!' And with that ironic socialist greeting, he hung up.

Perhaps one of the reasons why Prchal could behave so arrogantly was that he was not only on the Russians' pay-roll but was also an intimate of the then Czech president, Klement Gottwald, whom he visited daily but referred to as 'that drunken paralytic' behind his back.

(Incidentally when 'that drunken paralytic', or 'glorious helmsman, military commander and genius', as Stalin once publicly referred to him, died, his body was embalmed on the Russian model. But the workmanship was so bad that the body was in a permanent state of decomposition and had to be constantly re-opened so that more and more embalming fluid could be inserted!)

Another reason for Prchal's ability to abuse his power was that his boss, Minister of the Interior Bacilek, a fat, double-chinned long-time communist in his late fifties, was little better than senile. Once he had been a revolutionary—before the war he had attempted to blow up a tunnel and had been sent to jail because of it. Now his sole concern seemed to be his belly and military parades; he could spend hours, dressed in his general's uniform, watching the soldiers goose-step past him.

[1] Treason trials in the early '50's.

Normally he would come to work late, take off his too tight shoes and call for coffee and his 'secretary'. I don't know whether she could type or carry out the normal office routine. Perhaps not, for all that the Minister desired of her was that she commit fellatio on him while he read the morning intelligence resumés.

Prchal was well aware of the Minister's sexual peccadilloes and was continually making fun of his boss. When he received a recommendation from Bacilek that the secretary in question should be promoted to the rank of lieutenant, he sneered: 'She must have done it again for the old fart!'

And in those early years I learned one other vital fact about the strange new world into which I had been so innocently drawn—namely that our Soviet 'advisers'[1] were the real power behind the scenes. They even introduced the Czechs to the right kind of 'decor' for interrogation rooms! At the headquarters of the Bratislava Regional Directorate they had a cellar built, lined with white tiles. In its centre there was a butcher's block and next to it a masked executioner, complete with axe. At his feet stood a bucket of blood—animal not human—with which the walls had been liberally splashed. One sight of the executioner was usually enough for most 'suspects'. As one of the Czechs trained at Bratislava once told me, 'There, everybody confesses to everything!'

Until 1955, it was necessary to discuss every single action and every single proposal with the Soviet 'advisers'. They even controlled recruitment, not only from outside the service, but *within* it, from one branch of State Security to another. Obviously the Russians approved of me. Not only had they 'allowed' my fellow-countrymen to recruit me into the Service in the first place, but now, in late 1955, having been a minor member of one of the more obscure branches of the Service for nearly two years, they had approved my transfer to Counter-Intelligence.

Thus, still an enthusiastic young communist, believing passionately in the future of our new Republic—although a little more cynical about the men who ran it—I entered the strange, frightening, yet enormously exciting world of espionage. My apprenticeship was over; my war in the shadows had begun.

[1] It is sometimes thought by Westerners that *all* Eastern intelligence services are *still* run by the Russians. This is not true; but there is a great deal of liaison. In those early days of the new Soviet-style Republic, however, the Russians were indeed the real power in the Czech Service.

TWO

Early Operations

'Operation Kamen', the brainchild of Colonel Prchal, was one of the most ingenious and heartless intelligence 'plays' ever carried out, and one which I could not help admiring for its skilled execution, however much I abhorred its purpose.

It started in the early 'fifties when large numbers of Czechs wanted to leave their native land for political reasons. But in those days the State Security Services were not handing out exit visas. How, then, were these unfortunate people, who were really 'voting with their feet' and sacrificing everything they held dear to do so, going to get out? They would have to have recourse to the professional 'human smugglers', of which there have always been plenty in Central Europe, with its ever-changing régimes and political philosophies.

Prchal soon realized that one way to discover dissidents in Czechoslovakia was to find the professional 'human smugglers'. Then he had a brainwave. Why not recruit his own smugglers? He took the idea a step further. How were the potential escapers going to contact the smugglers—men they would normally not know, being usually law-abiding citizens? Naturally, through the 'resistance' movement. So he created a 'resistance movement' of his own.

Thus the plan was born. But before it was finally put into operation, Prchal added a brilliant refinement. With the aid of the 'resistance movement' and the professional smugglers, he would naturally be able to catch a large number of would-be escapers. But Prchal wanted more. He wanted to know *everybody* in Czechoslovakia who was disloyal to the State. Why not, then, find some way of making the escapers talk about those they had left behind? His answer to that problem was really brilliant. *He created a piece of West Germany within Czechoslovakia's own borders!*

In effect, the scheme worked like this. Led by the professional smuggler through the heavily wooded country that borders the lonely 'Bavarian Wood' area of West Germany, the would-be escapers crossed the border to be met by the West German *Grenzschutz,*[1] who after some delay would hand them over to the agents of the US CIC, the American Military Intelligence organization. Now the would-be escapers were taken to the 'American camp', where they were regaled with Bourbon and American cigarettes, before being questioned in offices draped with the Stars and Stripes and photographs of the current commander of the US Seventh Army. Relaxed and happy to have 'escaped', the unfortunate Czechs would blurt out their illegal activities 'back home', implicating many others still 'trapped' in the 'Workers' and Peasants' Republic'. Naturally there were a few who boasted of excessive illegal activities, which only existed in their imagination. They were going to regret their confidences bitterly a few hours later; for as soon as the interrogations were over, the CIC men dropped their faked American accents and revealed themselves as members of the Czech State Security Organization. The trials of these 'traitors' could now begin.

In the mid-'fifties Prchal added a new feature to his scheme, knowing that, if he stuck to the original too long, it would be compromised or betrayed somewhere along the line. The professional smuggler would hand his charges over to the CIC, who asked them to fill out questionnaires about their 'illegal' activities back in Czechoslovakia. Once this had been done, the escapers were herded into trucks to be driven deeper into 'West Germany'. Unfortunately, after only a few minutes' drive through the densely wooded countryside, the convoy would be 'ambushed' by units of the National Security Corps and both the escapers and their 'American' interrogators would be captured. Swiftly a trial was staged, in which not only were the questionnaires produced but also the supposedly crestfallen and scared 'CIC agents', only too eager to give evidence against the Czechs in order 'to save their own necks'. That *authentic* evidence usually clinched the case against the would-be escapers. Thus, if one of these unfortunate wretches ever did talk about his abortive escape, he would attribute its failure not to the 'resistance movement' but to the cunning of the National Security Corps.

[1] Border Guards.

Prchal, however, smart as he was, could not foresee all the possibilities inherent in Operation Kamen. Somewhere around mid-1955, one of the professional human smugglers belonging to the 'resistance movement' decided to go into business himself, while still officially working for Prchal. Located in the Pilsen area, he began to organize escapes off his own bat. Demanding exactly the same payment as the other Kamen operators—25,000 to 30,000 crowns—he would lead his hopeful, tense group of would-be escapers through the forests until they reached a tumble-down old forester's hut, where he ordered a break. Grateful for a rest after the tough going, the escapers would sink down on the ground. It was to be the last rest they would ever take. The guide then produced a sub-machine gun *and shot the lot of them in cold blood*!

Later, when the crime was discovered, investigating officers unearthed a mass grave on the site, filled with decomposing bodies. They were to discover more. On the smuggler's lonely border farm, they were searching the stables when they came across a grim sight. A filthy, half-naked 13-year-old Czech girl, who grinned at them insanely and shouted monstrous obscenities, was chained to the wall. The smuggler, a former member of the Czech National Socialist Party incidentally, had kept her tied up like this for months and had regularly raped her until the girl had gone out of her mind.

The smuggler was finally sentenced to death, but the macabre game on the frontier continued for several more years until Barak, the new Minister of State Security, finally stopped it.

In those years, while I was finding my feet as an intelligence man, Czechoslovakia was in the forefront of communist offensive intelligence operations against the West. Her only rival, East Germany, was not altogether trusted by the Soviet 'advisers', while her more cosmopolitan population and her geographical situation between East and West lent her obvious natural advantages. Thus it was left to the Czechs to try to carry out the mass 'poisoning' of the staff of Radio Free Europe in Munich. (See p. 33.) The Czechs also got the job of trying to bomb the same station's balloon base in West Germany, from whence balloons carrying leaflets were despatched towards the East. Incidentally, one such balloon collided with a Czech Ilyushin 14, flying close to the frontier, causing the plane to crash.

Even in Prague, where I was employed, we indulged in offensive operations. Our main targets were the foreign embassies, both from the Western countries and those of the so-called 'Third World'. Our aim was twofold—to prevent them from carrying out intelligence operations against Czechoslovakia; and, if we could, seduce, pervert, buy and blackmail their employees into working for us. Thus, everyone who entered the foreign embassies was checked and double-checked by the policeman standing at the gate (a member of the counter-intelligence service) and by the special surveillance team permanently on duty close by. If that weren't enough, every locally hired employee of the embassy was a member of our Intelligence, be he or she gardener or governess, telephonist or translator. Even the chimney sweeps, who checked the embassies' chimneys twice a year, were agents! Naturally the sweeps, like the Watergate 'plumbers', were very useful to us in checking whether our 'bugs' were still in place and in planting new ones. With the highly sophisticated equipment we were using even as far back as the mid-fifties, we knew more about the Ambassador's private life than his own First Secretary—down to how often he changed his socks or made love to his wife!

One operation in which I was involved at that time shows the lengths to which Czech Intelligence was prepared to go to compromise a foreigner and use him for their own purposes.

In the late 1950s a female employee of a foreign embassy in Prague came to the attention of Major Jan Koska, then head of one of our Security Departments and later Czech Consul in London (1962–7). The woman wasn't of diplomatic rank, but Koska thought she might prove useful if she could be compromised, and her life-style left her wide open to blackmail. Constant surveillance of her movements revealed that the lady, though middle-aged, liked young men, fast cars and alcohol—a dangerous combination at any time, but positively fatal for a diplomatic employee stationed in a communist country. Thus it was that a handsome young man was introduced into her life. It was love at first sight—at least on her part. The gigolo, naturally, was an employee of Koska's.

Koska allowed the affair to progress until he had a complete dossier on the woman's movements. Then he started the second phase of the operation. He ordered a rubber dummy! The dummy was made to look like an elderly man, dressed in shabby clothing.

Inside were plastic containers holding several litres of red liquid. It was also equipped with a spring mechanism attached to a cord, which activated the figure as if it were walking.

One evening the woman left for her usual rendezvous at the Hotel Hubertus some twenty miles from Prague, but, to her disappointment, the gigolo did not turn up. Just as she was about to get up from her table, the waiter brought the telephone. It was her boy friend; he couldn't make it that evening. That warranted another drink. Before she had finished it, a second young man appeared—also one of Koska's men—and introduced himself. They had a few drinks together, but just as she was beginning to get over her disappointment at the failed rendezvous, perhaps hoping she had found a substitute for the night, the stranger excused himself to go to the lavatory and didn't return.

Disillusioned at this second disappointment and slightly drunk, she clambered unsteadily into her car and, trying to forget her unsatisfactory evening, indulged herself in some dangerously fast driving. As she entered the suburb of Jiloviste she cut a corner a bit close and her headlights suddenly picked up the figure of an old man crossing the road. She jammed on the brakes but it was too late. With a sickening thud he hit the front bumper and fell to the ground, spurting blood everywhere.

Then, however, she did something which Koska and his pals, who were observing the scene from a convenient alley, had not bargained for. As the car went bump-bump over the dummy, she changed down, rammed her foot on the accelerator and took off as if the devil himself were after her. The Czech police gave chase, but the panic-stricken woman outpaced them. A traffic patrol tried to stop her but she plunged through them, scattering them wildly to left and right. Surprising the guard on the gate of her own Embassy, she was through it before he had a chance to react. Minutes later she was sobbing out what had happened to a senior official.

Forty-eight hours later she was flown out of Prague on her way home. Whether she was advised to do so by her Ambassador or whether she went of her own accord, I do not know. One thing is certain, however; until quite recently she believed that she had killed a man; the thought must have haunted her for years. In 1970, my account of the operation (which was passed to her) told her that she had merely run over a rubber dummy filled with red paint!

I only tell this somewhat ridiculous story in such detail to show the extraordinary lengths to which Czech Intelligence were prepared to go in order to compromise and thereafter subvert even the most insignificant members of the staffs of foreign embassies, and the elaborate, almost childish, situations which they saw fit to engineer.

THREE

Barak!

The man who had given the go-ahead for 'Operation Rubber Duck', as the blackmail attempt on the unfortunate lady was called, was the new star in the Czech Intelligence heaven— Minister of the Interior Rudolf Barak. A small, dark-haired man in his late thirties, Barak had come from the provinces to take over the Ministry after Bacilek's move* and it was clear from the start that a bold new element had entered our lives. As one colleague of mine said, 'Just look at that express train! But don't try to stop it, or it'll run you over!' They were to be prophetic words.

Almost immediately Barak began to get rid of those who were most compromised. The torturers and murderers were quietly dismissed or jailed, and those who had ordered them to carry out their foul deeds soon followed, including my own one-time chief, Prchal. Once Barak had got rid of these people, he set about making himself popular with the rank-and-file like myself. He went to every social event we held, mixing not with the senior officers but with the junior ones, drinking with them, telling dirty jokes, dancing with their wives. Nor did he toady to the scented Russian advisers as his predecessors had done. He was friendly enough to them, but that was all. Obviously he wanted to show that he wasn't in Russian pay and was first and foremost a Czech.

But he did more than just socialize with his subordinates. He saw they got pay increases, decent apartments and good cars, and that they were not forced to do unnecessary duties. On the other hand, he ensured that Intelligence was run more efficiently, cutting out corruption and useless duplication. He also made each officer undergo ten days' physical training at a special centre once a year—and naturally the Minister himself was first to attend the course. As a consequence our output and efficiency went up

* Bacilek had been elected First Secretary of the Slovak Communist Party.

almost overnight. Soon Barak was the most popular senior officer in Czech Intelligence—'a real democrat as well as a good communist', as one of my friends put it.

Yet it seemed to me even then that there was something more to Barak's activities than a straightforward attempt to improve the department's efficiency. For although, as I have said, he did not stand on his rank and was in no way vain, yet he was continually having photographs of himself with top Russians such as Khrushchev and Bulganin published in the Czech papers, almost as if he were trying to create the impression that the Russians had come to Prague to see him and not Novotny, the President.[1]

In addition, he made his head of economic counter-intelligence, Colonel Rybin, concentrate not on attempts to sabotage the national economy of capitalist countries (which should have been his job) but on the deficiencies in the management of our *own* economy. In other words, the Colonel's task was to spy on his own Government!

Barak also indulged in activities which hadn't the remotest thing to do with the work of the Ministry. He encouraged painters and writers. He encouraged sport and had a beautiful sports arena built in Prague—the only one in the country. He founded the Red Star Hockey Club, as well as two football clubs of the same name. But strangest of all was his obsession with the part his fellow-countrymen had played in the war.

On a visit to Moscow he persuaded Khrushchev to send a notorious double-agent called Nachtmann back to Czechoslovakia. During the war Nachtmann had been a senior member of the Gestapo in Prague, an anti-communist 'expert', and in charge of operations against Czech resistance, a man who had many honest Czechs on his conscience. *At the same time, Nachtmann had been a Soviet spy!*[2]

To what use, I asked myself at the time, could Barak want to put such a swine as Nachtmann, whose activities were well known even to me.

---

[1] He made the chief censor, an employee of the Intelligence Service, cut out all photos except those of himself!

[2] My own post-war researches in Czech Intelligence files showed me that Nachtmann and Commissar Leimer were the key Soviet spies within the Gestapo. Leimer was promoted to NKVD Colonel after the war. Their assignment was to destroy non-communist resistance, supposedly for Germany, but in reality to further Russia's post-war plans in Central Europe.

And Nachtmann was not the only figure from the past who seemed to fascinate Barak. There was Johann Siebert, a prematurely aged ex-member of the German SD,[1] serving a life-sentence in Leopoldov Prison. On Barak's orders, Siebert was spirited out of prison, given some rejuvenation surgery, the cover name of Danilo, a comfortable apartment, an allowance and a new identity as a rug salesman. From an aged 'lifer' Siebert was suddenly transformed into a middle-aged businessman with plenty of money, who had the ear of the Minister of State Security himself.

Why? Because Danilo was not only a walking index of wartime Czech and German agents within the country, but had also come up with the suggestion that, as all agents were paid and as the Germans are a notoriously thorough people, they would have kept the financial records of those payments. Immediately a search was instituted and within three weeks the files were found in the archives of Prague's National Bank. They contained 70,000 names—and what names they were![2]

Lastly, Barak gave an even more extraordinary example of his obsession with a past that most people in Czechoslovakia only wanted to forget. He issued orders that a man whom most people had thought long dead, be found. That man was Gestapo Müller!

SS General Heinrich Müller, an ex-Bavarian policeman, who prior to 1933 was both a rabid anti-communist *and* anti-Nazi, had been appointed head of the Gestapo on Heydrich's order in spite of the opposition of the local Munich branch of the Nazi Party. (Up to 1939, Heydrich wasn't even a Nazi himself.) In the late 'thirties Müller came to Berlin and built the Gestapo into the powerful force which, after the outbreak of war, was to spread terror through all the occupied countries.

But Müller was nothing if not a realist and as soon as it became apparent that Germany was going to lose the war he seemed to change sides. At least, that is what SS General Schellenberg thought.[3] Be that as it may, when everyone else of importance in his department was fleeing from Berlin, Müller decided to stay

---

[1] The SS's Intelligence Service, headed by General Schellenberg during the war.

[2] One which caused me a great deal of personal grief, and made a lasting impression on me, was that of my beloved uncle who had 'suffered' so much in Nazi camps. In fact he had been a Gestapo spy!

[3] See Schellenberg's memoirs for further details of his conversation with Müller on the subject in 1943.

behind. It was Schellenberg's theory that Müller, accompanied only by a radio operator, stayed behind in the cellar of the shattered Gestapo HQ in order to go over to the Russians, with whom he was already in radio contact. At all events when Müller's 'grave' was dug up in Berlin in the early 'sixties, it was found to contain the bones of three much younger men! Where, then, was Gestapo Müller?

According to my informant within Czech Intelligence, this is what happened. In 1955 Müller was discovered living under an assumed name in South America. Instead of informing the South American authorities or the Germans, who still had a warrant out for Müller's arrest, Barak determined to kidnap Müller off his own bat and bring him to Czechoslovakia. An agent living in France was given the job and, just as the Israelis kidnapped Eichmann, Müller was smuggled aboard a ship heading for Szczecin (Stettin). From there he was transferred to a jail in Czechoslovakia where he was allowed special privileges on the undertaking that he wouldn't breathe a word about his real identity, even to the chief jailer. He didn't speak Czech anyway.

Thus, if my informant was correct, Barak now had three key Nazis at his disposal, complete with comprehensive records of nearly all known wartime German agents within Czechoslovakia. But why? For the time being the question had to remain unanswered. For I, too, had become strangely involved in the past.

The business had begun on a freezing cold night in late April, 1942, when Czech paras landed in a remote and lonely part of occupied Czechoslovakia. They were one of several teams flown into the country on instructions from the British as part of the operation which led eventually to the assassination of SS General Reinhard Heydrich. The team was later betrayed and one of its members, a 21-year-old Czech Army lieutenant named Vaclav Kindl, changed sides under threat of death, and became a Gestapo agent. Under the direction of Willy Leimer, the Gestapo's communist expert who, as we have seen, was also a major in the NKVD, Kindl played an important role in 'Operation Hermelin', a radio game with London, which entailed luring Czech para agents into German traps, thus preventing the Government-in-Exile from giving aid to the resistance movement, which Leimer and his Russian masters naturally wanted to destroy.

In 1944 a trap was set for one such agent and Kindl was brought along by Leimer to identify him. But the agent decided to shoot it out. In the mêlée Kindl was *apparently* seriously wounded and taken to hospital, where he died. (His gravestone records that he was shot by the Gestapo.) Thus, seemingly, Kindl, the traitor, had suffered his deserved fate.

But one day, over ten years later, Kindl's sister received a strange letter from a certain V. Nodat in London, saying that he had known Kindl, and enclosing a photograph showing Kindl in the uniform of the Free Czech Army. The correspondence, which was one-sided because Nodat gave no address, continued for some time, until the sister confided in a friend who, unknown to her, was one of our agents. She immediately notified State Security and thus I became involved in the case.

It didn't take me long to realize that the spirit of the long-dead Kindl was being heard through the medium of the strange Mr Nodat. But to what purpose? Finally I decided to visit the surgeon who had allegedly tried to save Kindl's life that night in 1944 after the shoot-out with the para agent. I took with me a set of photographs, including those of Kindl and Leimer. I showed some of the pictures to the surgeon and he said that none of them was of the man he had operated on. I then showed him Kindl's photo. 'Was this the man?' I asked.

'Of course not,' he replied instantly. 'That's Vaclav Kindl.'

I hid my surprise just in time. 'How do you know?'

'We were at military academy together.'

I realized at once that the mysterious Mr Nodat was Kindl himself. But what was he doing in London? I never found the answer to that question. Was Leimer, in Moscow, or Leimer's successors, still working him as an 'illegal'? I don't know. Perhaps he had settled down in Britain as just another 'bloody foreigner'— one more elderly exile from his native country, reading obscure newspapers and eating strange foods, living from one meeting of his local Czech Club to the next. Again I don't know. Nor did the British MI5, who sought him actively in the early 'seventies, as soon as they had interrogated me after my defection.[1]

[1] I did find out later that his death had been faked by Leimer. Thereafter he had entered the Foreign Legion. On demobilization in 1950, with a new identity, he had gone to London, where some kind of homesickness had compelled him to write to his one surviving relative. Both she and his mother had been in German concentration camps during the war.

But if my excursion into the past proved purposeless, my superior's did not. It was to provide him with a brief triumph, now that he had all the trumps up his sleeve, and an equally rapid downfall that would see him in prison for 'life'.

FOUR

The Downfall of Rudolf Barak

The discovery of Barak's scheme and his subsequent arrest started innocently enough. In 1960 President Novotny paid a visit to the United Nations in New York and the local representatives of Czech Intelligence decided to give the President a gift—typical of the sort of toadying that went on all the time. But before they had decided what to buy with the money they had collected, the President had already returned to Czechoslovakia.

Some time later Novotny, a man well known for feathering his own nest, remembered about the proposed gift and asked that the money should be transferred to Prague. This simple request caused consternation in New York; for Barak, then the second most powerful man in the State, had already sequestrated the cash, a gesture symptomatic of his profound contempt for Novotny. But that did not help his alarmed subordinates in New York, and in the end one of their number, an unscrupulous Major named Necvalec, simply drew the money from the Intelligence Service's secret funds and issued it in Novotny's name. There the matter would have ended had not Necvalec decided that this seemed to be an excellent way of milking the fund on his own account, using the President's name. Thus, over the next few months, he started dipping his fingers in the till.

But he had reckoned without a diligent accountant named Major Skala, who started to query the numerous sums of money paid over to Novotny. Finally he went to the President himself, his accountant's heart made bold by this apparent abuse of public funds. Novotny fell into a tremendous rage when he discovered where the original money had gone. But his anger was not directed at the accountant, nor even at Major Necvalec. It was directed at Barak for having used the original money for his own purposes. The break between the President and his Second-in-Command was about to come into the open at last.

Novotny had known for some time what the real purpose behind Barak's unsentimental journeys into the past was. Here and there his own spies in Intelligence had let a word slip, revealed an odd incident, hinted at their suspicions that key Nazis from the days of the Occupation were being hidden by Barak. And it hadn't taken Novotny long to guess what Barak was up to—he was about to make a bid for power himself by revealing the truth about Novotny's past!

During the war Novotny, an active member of the illegal Communist Party, had been arrested and sent to Mauthausen concentration camp. Here he had become a *Kapo*, a trusty, one of those who would survive because they had better food, medical treatment, less work—even sex, if they wanted it, in the camp's brothel. How did one become a *Kapo*? The answer was simple: one became a spy for the Gestapo. And that is exactly what Novotny did. He revealed all he knew about his illegal organization back home, as well as what was going on within the camp itself. This was the information Barak had been after on his strange excursions into the past. So now Novotny decided that he must use Barak's appropriation of the New York money to get rid of him before Barak had time to release his bombshell, which must surely end Novotny's own career.

At the next meeting of the Politburo, the top committee of the Czech Communist Party, Novotny accused Barak of misusing state funds, his fat face flushing as he explained what had happened in New York. At first the other members of the Politburo were at a loss to know how to react. The friendship between Barak and Novotny was considered to be unshakeable. Then they tumbled to what was going on and were forced to decide whom they would support. They chose Novotny. He was relatively harmless, whereas Barak was dangerous and knew too much about every one of them.

A few minutes later a now enraged Barak told them just exactly how much he knew. Swinging round at Simunek, he shouted, 'You have ruined the whole Czech economy with your poor planning,' and went on to tell the ex-shoe polish maker that in addition to being a lousy economist, he had a brother who was working in England for the British Secret Intelligence Service. 'With that kind of background, Simunek,' he bellowed, 'you shouldn't even be given a job as a patrolman in Public Security!'

Then he turned on Koutsky, another high-ranking member of the Politburo, and reminded him of how he had once been a 'very close friend' of Nachtmann and Leimer. 'You were only released from prison in 1945 on the charge of collaboration because there was insufficient evidence against you. But I could produce that evidence any time I want!' One by one, he revealed their unsavoury pasts and presents—how they had worked for the Gestapo, done deals on the black market, revealed the top secrets of the new Czech state to the KGB and so on—until finally he turned on Novotny himself. 'And you,' he shouted, 'you'd better be quiet or I can tell one or two things about you which you wouldn't like to be discussed in public!'

Novotny tried to appease him. 'Rudy,' he said, 'I'm not accusing you! We don't do that sort of thing at these meetings. All I wanted to know was what had happened to the money in New York.'

In the end Barak let himself be appeased. The meeting turned to another subject and ended half an hour later. But the die had been cast. Novotny knew now that Barak could not be allowed to enjoy his freedom any longer. As soon as the meeting broke up and Barak had gone, Novotny summoned another one. Within minutes the Politburo members had voted for the immediate arrest of Rudolf Barak!

That evening two Colonels in State Security went to Barak's home to arrest him, but once again Barak used his knowledge of the past to outwit his enemies. He reminded one of the officers of how he had been a Gestapo spy during the war, which gave the man such a shock that he was physically ill afterwards. The other was also known to Barak and he then started to get cold feet, so that in the end they left, without having arrested Barak and the Minister shouting at them triumphantly, 'And remember I have immunity from arrest as long as I am a member of the National Assembly.'

Crestfallen, the Colonels reported back to Novotny, who had every single member of the National Assembly roused from their beds at three o'clock in the morning and forced them to dismiss Barak from the Assembly.

But Barak wasn't beaten yet. Next day he was confronted by Novotny and Strougal, once Minister of Agriculture, now Minister of the Interior. In silence Barak listened to the charge and then asked to see the order for his arrest. His trained eye spotted at once that it had not been signed by the Prosecutor-General, which was necessary to make it legal. Contemptuously, he tossed it back to Strougal. 'Here, Lubomir,' he said, 'you should know that you can't arrest anyone without the order of the Prosecutor-General.'

But Novotny was too deeply involved to back out now. 'Of course, I can arrest you without his signature,' he declared. 'And as First Secretary (of the Politburo) I'm expelling you from the Party.'

So Barak was arrested, while Novotny frantically sought for evidence that Barak had indeed been planning a *coup d'état* against him. But even the most servile prosecutor would not accept the 'evidence' he had prepared. Novotny then made the charge financial. Believing in the old adage that if you're going to lie, lie big, he accused Barak of stealing 75,000 US dollars from government funds for his own use. It was a total fabrication; and everyone in Intelligence knew that the money had been used to finance one of our undercover ops. Indeed the money was only found in Barak's safe *after two previous searches in which the investigating officers had virtually taken Barak's office apart*! In other words, Novotny had had the money planted in the safe.

But it did the trick and poor Barak who, long before Dubcek, might have transformed Czechoslovakia into a more democratic country, was sent off to serve a life sentence of solitary confinement. His career was over and in a very indirect manner the stage was being set for those terrible events which were to happen to my poor country eight years later.[1]

The Barak affair played an important role in my spiritual development at that time. When I became aware of the full details, which weren't too hard to find out in my somewhat privileged position, I realized just how corrupt and power-crazy the Old

[1] Barak survived to be released, a broken man, in the 'Prague Spring' of 1968. Today he is a filling station attendant in some obscure suburban garage.
Major Necvalec, who had caused his downfall, was killed several years later in a car accident. Strangely enough his identity card showed him to be a colonel in Intelligence, though he had been dismissed years before with the rank of major. Obviously Novotny had promoted him for services rendered during the Barak affair.

Guard of Communists then ruling Czechoslovakia really were. All of them were compromised. In 1942 Gestapo Müller had once remarked to General Schellenberg, 'After all the whole Czech underground is financed and directed, on the one hand by the British, and on the other by Moscow.' Very true—but he might have added, in the light of what Barak's researches had revealed, *by the Gestapo as well*!

Nearly all the old men who ruled Czechoslovakia had sold their comrades and fellow Czechs, especially if they belonged to the bourgeois parties, to the enemy in order to save their own lives. Yet these same men talked with apparently genuine disgust of 'treachery to the young Republic' and demanded unconditional loyalty from the millions of young Czechs who served their country in the naive belief that it had broken completely with the corruption and double-dealing of the past. Brave New World indeed!

But there was more to the Barak Affair than just the dirty revelations about a handful of nasty old men. For me it had a wider and more shocking significance. For Barak's discoveries had shown to what lengths the Russians would go to further the advance, not of Communism, but of Soviet Imperialism. There was no better word for it.

Nachtmann and Leimer and all their Czech helpers, such as my once revered uncle, had deliberately used their role in the Gestapo, while in fact they were officers of the NKVD, to wipe out all bourgeois resistance. Hundreds of Czechs went to their deaths during the war in the belief that they were dying a hero's death fighting the enemy. In fact they were being sacrificed by an ally, a cold-blooded, calculating ally, whose major concern was not the defeat of the enemy but the establishment of a sound local basis for the take-over of the country which they were supposed to be fighting to liberate!

In the light of the above, the reader might well ask why did I not leave the Service in 1960, after I had learned the full extent of Barak's disclosures. I was still free to go. Naturally I had learned some state secrets during the last eight years, but nothing so terrible, I suppose, that my own Service might have been forced to stop my mouth—for good. Certainly, with what I knew, I would never have been allowed to leave Czechoslovakia. Naturally, today, I could plead that no other career was then open to me. I had long since forgotten most of what I had once known about accountancy and office administration. Besides, I was now married and had a young son (today, incidentally, a complete young American and the pride of his high school's karate club). How would I provide for my family without a steady job?

But that would have only been an excuse. The truth was more complex. I had fallen a victim to the drug of espionage, which is just as potent, all-consuming and dangerous as the real thing. The war in the shadows, with its heady excitements and dangers, had entered my soul. After eight years in the Service, I could not visualize any other life, even though I knew it was being used to bolster up a corrupt and cruel régime. I had to have the constant stimulus of new ops, intrigue, blackmail, the deadly chess game of espionage; and I had succumbed to what Charles Whiting in his book *The War in the Shadows* aptly calls the 'key-hole complex'. I *had* to know what was going on on the other side of the door. I *had* to know who were the men in foreign Intelligence who carried out policies totally contrary to those put forward by their 'front office'. I *had* to know the dirt: who were the womanizers, the homosexuals, the financial crooks, the blackmail victims. In short, by 1960 I was caught. There could be no other life for me.

And now, as Barak started his long, lonely sentence in some provincial prison, my superiors increased my ration of the deadly espionage drug. They transferred me to the British desk of Czech Intelligence. I was going on active operations at last.

The British Desk (1960–1964)

ONE

The Lonsdale Plot

I was recruited into the élite branch of Czech Intelligence by an old pal of mine, Major Jaroslav Nemec, who had been a friend since childhood. Born into a poor mining family, he had entered Intelligence in 1948, being posted to the German section, and for most of his career he was concerned with the German-language area—Germany, Austria and Switzerland.

It was because of his preoccupation with things German that he turned up again in Prague—at a very opportune moment for me. I had already made several applications for a transfer to active Intelligence and had been turned down; he gave me the vital sponsorship I needed.

It happened like this. Nemec had decided that he was going to silence, if only for a little while, the stream of anti-communist propaganda coming from the American-sponsored Radio Free Europe, and so, from his cover-post in the Czech consulate in Salzburg, he set up a small ring of agents in Munich, whose task was to 'poison' the station's employees by placing potassium cyanide crystals in the salt cellars used in the cafeteria—a typical Nemec scheme. Unfortunately for Nemec, and very fortunately for the unsuspecting employees, it misfired because one of his agents was also working for American Intelligence. Immediately a warrant was issued by the Viennese police for Nemec's arrest, whereupon the Czechs panicked. Nemec did not have a diplomatic passport. If he were arrested and charged, it would result in serious political trouble. Nemec had to be removed from Austria immediately. But he could not be found. Then one of the men looking for him, a certain Molnar, remembered that Nemec had a favourite inn in the Tyrolean Alps. He drove to the inn to find Nemec, sitting with four Austrian gendarmes, all of them blind drunk and singing dirty songs!

Molnar wasted no time on explanations. Shoving Nemec outside, he put him in his car and drove like a madman for the nearest frontier, stopping only to stuff him into the boot so that he could smuggle him across. Thus Nemec turned up once more in my life and helped to secure me the post I had long coveted.

The Czechoslovak Intelligence Service had (and still has) a special status and was considered to be the aristocrat of all the Communist Intelligence services. The legitimate descendant of the famed pre-war and wartime Czech Intelligence, which had operated from London between 1939 and 1945, it had remained a relatively small department until 1950. Then the situation changed drastically. Under Russian influence, it grew to mammoth proportions, considering the size of Czechoslovakia. Its budget was tremendous. Most of the diplomatic staff at every Czech embassy and consulate throughout the world were its employees. In my time in London, for instance, only four of the personnel were *not* members of Czech Intelligence. It also had a considerable illegal network in every 'target' country approved by the Russians.

Thus I was a very proud man when I was accepted into the service in October, 1960 and entered my office on the third floor of the 'Old Building', as it was called, which had a panoramic view of Prague and which, incidentally, looked out across the river at the British Embassy, the official Czech 'home' of my own 'target' country.[1]

I still had a lot to learn, although I had already been in various forms of counter-intelligence for eight years. As Nemec, the old hand, now busy once again trying to find some means of eliminating his particular *bête noire*, Radio Free Europe, said, 'Don't worry Josef; you're going to fall flat on your big face a couple of times before you find your feet in this particular business!' How right he was.

One morning in the spring of 1961 a routine batch of entry visa applications landed on my desk. At that time my country was encouraging tourism and a lot of Westerners were visiting Czechoslovakia. But while the Ministry of Trade, who were responsible for tourism, was thus engaged, Intelligence did not stop its scrutiny of the new visitors; every one of them was a potential recruit for our own service.

[1] Originally I was intended for the West German desk but because I spoke English I was transferred almost immediately to the British desk.

So, I began the boring job of going through the applications, consoling myself with the thought that as the 'new boy' I had to do the donkey work. One, however, held my attention. Each application had the seals of counter-intelligence and the criminal police on the back, certifying that the person in question had already been checked out by those two services. This one, made out by an Englishman called Mr Mark, had a note on it, stating that a file already existed on him. I was curious, so I went along to our archives and discovered that Mark had been a security officer at the British Embassy across the river in the late 'forties. After marrying a Czech girl from the town of Louny, he had returned to England and had become a warder at Pentonville Prison. Nothing startling, but as the man was married to a Czech and had visited his wife's native country several times in the last few years, I thought it might be useful to suggest to Taborsky, my chief, that Mark should be contacted as a potential agent.

Two days later I was summoned by Taborsky, who was in a great state of excitement. The senior Russian adviser to our service, Colonel Litvinov, wanted to see me personally! So, a little nervously, I reported to the KGB man whose 'advice' was law within my department. Litvinov was as excited as my own chief.

Tapping my report on Mark, he asked, 'Did you write this, Frolik?'

'Yes, Comrade Colonel.'

'And do you know it's importance?'

'I can guess it, Comrade Colonel, though the Englishman is only a humble prison guard. But you obviously know more.'

'Yes, but at what prison?'

'Pentonville,' I said.

'And do you know who is imprisoned there?'

I shook my head.

Litvinov allowed himself a faint smile.

'Comrade Kanon Timofievich Molody!'

I swallowed hard. What a fool I had been not to have realized Mr Mark's importance myself. He was charged with guarding none other than Russia's arch-spy, Gordon Lonsdale!

Molody, alias Lonsdale, had come to England on a Canadian passport in 1955 and ran an interesting KGB spy-ring, centred principally on the Krogers, the radio operators, working from their bungalow at Ruislip in Middlesex, and Harry Houghton and Ethel Gee, his mistress, the active spies at Portland naval base.

For four years all had gone well. Lonsdale had occupied himself with a series of nubile young mistresses under the cover of selling bubble-gum machines and juke-boxes, while Houghton and his mistress kept him well supplied with information about the Admiralty Underwater Weapons Establishment at Portland.

In 1960, however, things had started to go wrong. Lonsdale's business went into liquidation with liabilities of £30,000 and the Portland Naval Security Officer started to take an interest in Harry Houghton, who had access to the latest developments in the top-secret underwater radar research being carried out at Portland. MI5 had been called in to check Houghton's movements—he was obviously spending much more than he was earning—and they soon discovered that virtually every Saturday afternoon, Houghton met Lonsdale, usually carrying some kind of parcel.

On Saturday afternoon, 7 January, 1961, Superintendent George Smith of the Special Branch, an old-time spy catcher, stopped Lonsdale, Houghton and Gee near the Old Vic. At his subsequent interrogation in Scotland Yard, Lonsdale maintained a stony silence after saying with a smile, 'To any question you might ask me, my answer is "No".' Two months later, on 18 March, 1961, Russia's master spy in Britain was sentenced to twenty-five years' imprisonment.[1] This was the man with whom I happened to have discovered a link, right on our own doorstep, and it more than explained my chief's and Colonel Litvinov's excitement. Suddenly, completely out of the blue, tremendous possibilities had been opened up.

Litvinov laid it on the line straight away: 'Frolik, we are not interested in any formal permanent co-operation with this Englishman. All we wish is that the Czech Service recruit him—

---

[1] On 21 April, 1964, Lonsdale was exchanged for Greville Wynne, a British Intelligence agent who had served eleven months of an eight-year sentence for spying in the Soviet Union. Back in Russia, Lonsdale became the star of a film called *The Dead Season* which closely followed his career in espionage in the West. On 14 October, 1970, it was announced in Moscow that he had died while picking mushrooms in the country. He was 48.

The Krogers got 20 years apiece, Houghton and Miss Gee 15. They are all free now. The Krogers were last heard of in Lublin in Poland, where Peter Kroger is employed in the English Department of the University.

money is no object, you can have £100,000 if you wish—for one single operation to help us spring Comrade Molody.'

We started planning the operation at once. Taborsky was full of enthusiasm. 'We've got to pull it off for the honour of the Czech Service,' he urged several times, obviously out to impress our Russian adviser. Relieving me of all other duties, he gave me my first contact and told me to get on with it. The contact was Captain V. Salac, Mark's brother-in-law, an officer in charge of a battalion of internal security guards at the chemical factory at Zaluzi near the town of Most.

Immediately I began to check out his record. It was excellent. He was described by his superiors as a high-grade officer who was a member of the Communist Party. There was only one omission in his record—he had never told our own counter-intelligence that he had a sister married to a member of the British Security Services (as we regarded prison warders). I was not particularly concerned about this 'oversight'. But the Major who did the checking on Salac for me hit the ceiling. He demanded that Salac should be charged immediately with having committed an act of active espionage. In the end I had to bring the big guns to bear on him, in the shape of Colonel Litvinov, to get him off my back. He went off in a huff, but unfortunately I hadn't heard the last of the irate Major.

I contacted Salac, who proved to be very co-operative. He agreed to visit his sister, Mrs Mark, as soon as she arrived back home and make a certain financial proposition to her in order to attempt to subvert her husband.

'They don't pay well in London,' he said carefully. 'What if I offered her a thousand pounds? Or is that too much?'

I laughed. 'You can offer her a hundred thousand pounds if she can convince her husband to work with us.'

Salac looked at me as if I were raving mad. A few days later we met again and Salac filled me in about his brother-in-law's financial state—his big mortgage, his desire to buy a new car, his dislike of his poorly paid job, etc. In my turn, I told Salac what we needed to know from Mark—copies of cell keys, plans of the jail, the location of Lonsdale's cell, the types of security devices used, and so on. When we parted that afternoon, I was quietly confident that Salac would do his best to recruit his brother-in-law.

But I had reckoned without the counter-intelligence Major. He contacted Salac behind my back and found out what the great mystery was about. When the confused and, no doubt, worried Salac had finished his story, the Major pulled a long face and said, 'You know this is a very serious matter. You'd better prepare yourself for the worst, Captain. We can't employ people like you in the Service. After all, your brother-in-law is not only British, he's employed by the British Government.' Picking up his cap he rose to his feet with a final warning: 'You'll be hearing from me in due course.'

Captain Salac, now scared out of his wits, took the only step he thought open to him. He took his brother-in-law, who had just arrived, for a walk in the country, where he could not be overheard. He didn't tell Mark the whole story but enough to get him really worried. His advice to his brother-in-law was to 'get out of the country as quick as you can'.

That same afternoon we picked Salac up. He confessed immediately that he had warned his brother-in-law. Desperately I tried to think up some new ploy. But it was too late. Even before I could get to Salac's sister's house, Mark and his wife were on their way back to England, driving through the night at top speed for the nearest frontier. Poor Salac was transferred to a humdrum job and the interfering Major was demoted. But their punishment didn't mean much to me, as my dreams of great glory—'the man who rescued Lonsdale'—disappeared down the drain.

TWO

The Heath Caper

During my early years at the British desk, one of the most interesting of our men at the Czech Embassy in London was Major Mrazek, who used the cover name of Ptacek. Ptacek had lived in London a long time and he had fallen completely for the English way of life. Unlike his colleagues, who took to English habits of necessity, he really loved the country and its life style. He gave up coffee for tea. He spoke English fluently with a very upper-class accent. He was a frequent visitor to the House of Commons and a welcome guest in many 'smart' British homes, where he was known simply as 'John', a friend from behind the Iron Curtain and certainly the most unlikely Communist the aristocratic English had ever met. Even the doors of Cabinet Ministers were open to him!

At one time he was very 'friendly' with the wife of a certain Minister who will have to remain nameless because of Britain's rigid libel laws. (Often I think they are as effective in preventing the truth from being told as any Iron Curtain censor's blue pencil.) So much so that he made an application to Prague for official permission to seduce the lady, with a view to blackmailing her later for intelligence purposes. In Communist States such things are taken seriously and have to be the subject of a high-power conference, where the pros and cons are solemnly considered by high-ranking officers.

For a change, however, John's suggestion must have been received by a humorist. Knowing that his potency as a lover was not what it had been, he cabled back: 'Request rejected! Question applicant's ability to perform. Remember the honour of the Czech nation is at stake!'

It was a story that was still going the rounds years later when I was posted to the London Embassy. But John took it in good heart. As long as he was permitted to remain in his beloved London he didn't care what nameless officers in Prague thought of his sexual prowess.

However, John was no fool. He had excellent contacts in London society and was always on the look-out for likely candidates. Thus, one day when he suggested that we might take a closer look at an up-and-coming Conservative politician, who was still unmarried although he was pushing fifty and apparently did not indulge in sexual high jinks on the side, we gave the man in question serious consideration. Thus the Heath Caper was born.

In essence, John had formed the opinion that Mr Heath was not markedly heterosexually inclined. From our studies of the British establishment, we knew that several prominent politicians, generals, admirals, judges and so forth were homosexual, although security precautions in this area had been tightened up a great deal after the Burgess and Maclean defections. In this case John had no evidence on which to base his assumptions but it seemed worth a try. And so we started to plan an elaborate scheme to entice Mr Heath to come to Czechoslovakia. Once there, we would spring a trap on him which would leave him, so we hoped, wide open to blackmail, so that when he returned to his own country, he would be forced to act in our interest, feeding us top-level information.

Some readers of the above might find it nauseating. But let me assure them that blackmail of this kind is an important tool in the arsenal of intelligence services on both sides of the Iron Curtain. Other, less cynical, readers might argue that a senior politician would not leave himself open to such blackmail. Let me assure them that senior politicians, when driven by their sexual urges, leave themselves just as vulnerable to blackmail as any erring husband out having a 'fling' or homosexual 'hustling' in some back-street lavatory. Thus, when I was in London four years later, my colleagues were 'running' one Labour Minister who was a homosexual as well as being greedy for money, and were well aware that another leading politician of another party had left himself wide open to approach because of his homosexual inclinations. (We failed to recruit him, may I add.)

Under normal circumstances, my Department had a good number of young men and women at our disposal, willing and

40

1. Gordon Lonsdale, the 'Portland Spy' who was sentenced to 25 years' imprisonment in 1961 but was later exchanged for Greville Wynne.

2. Antonin Novotny, President of the Czechoslovak Republic from 1957 to 1968.

3. Josef Frolik with his wife and son on Westminster Bridge in 1964 when he was working in London.

Mrs Frolik in England, Winter, 1964.

5. Frolik's son outside the block of flats in Bayswater Road in which he lived from 1964 to 1966.

6. Josef Josten, Director of the Free Czech Information News Agency.

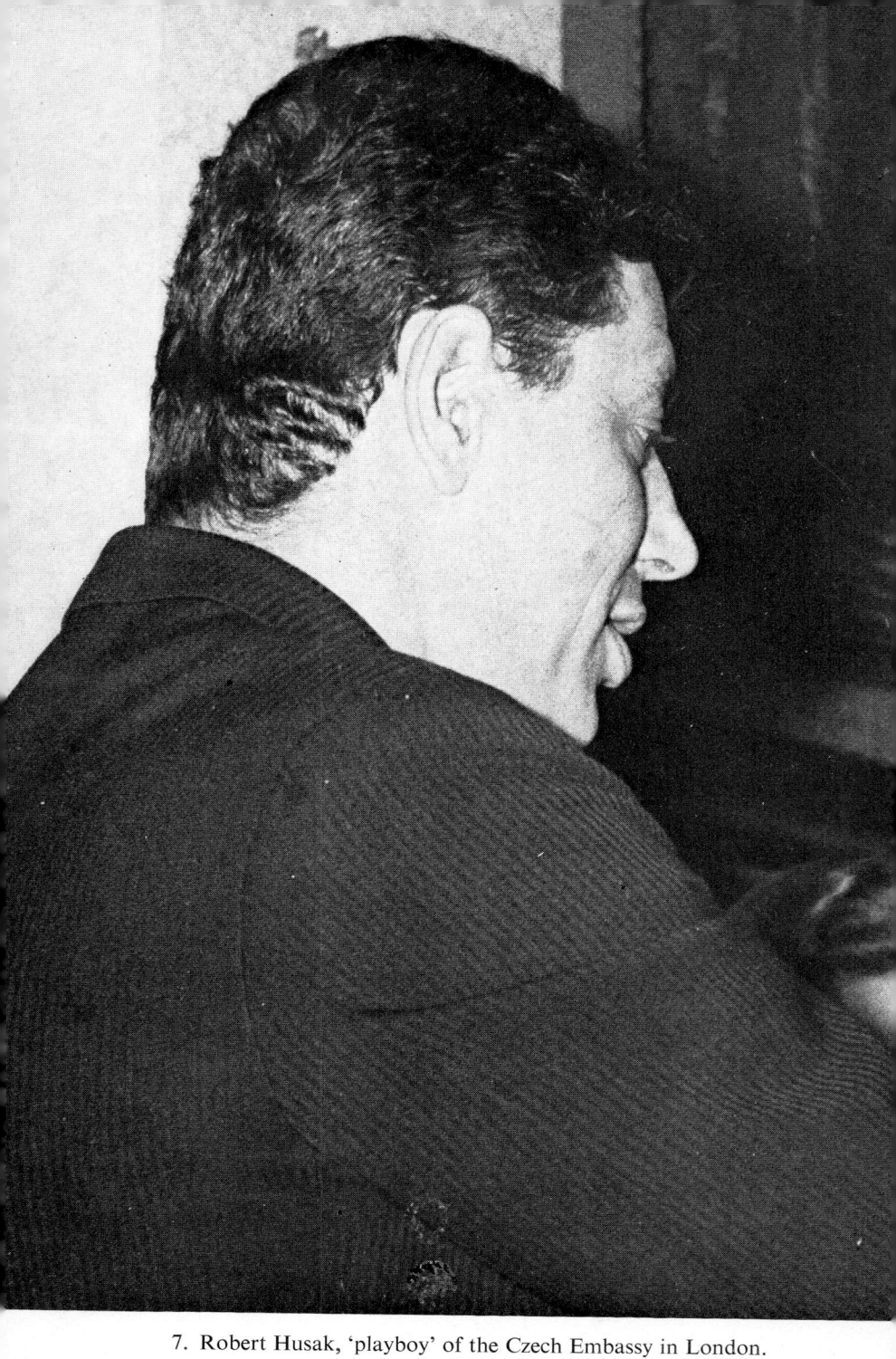

7. Robert Husak, 'playboy' of the Czech Embassy in London.

able to carry out any kind of sexual practice, from normal hetero and homosexual seduction through the standard deviations such as flagellation, up to the most *outré* forms of voyeurism. In this case, we did not want to use any of the more obvious forms of sexual seduction. Our man would have to attract his victim on a completely normal basis. If John's suppositions turned out to be correct, then 'Mr X' could apply his charms. If they turned out wrong, 'Mr X' could still establish a useful basis of understanding through some form of common bond or interest.

Again it was John who supplied us with that interest. Mr Heath, he informed us, was a gifted amateur musician. (Those were in the days before he started to acquire the more rugged image of a sailor.) In particular, he was very keen on playing the organ. Immediately we set out to look for a Czech organist who might fit the bill. We found him in the person of Professor Jaroslav Reinberger, a handsome organ virtuoso, who lived in Brno, the capital of Moravia. Not only did Professor Reinberger have bisexual inclinations (we already had a file on him) but he actually knew Mr Heath.

Reinberger was contacted at once. What means were used to make him agree to become part of the plot, I do not know. But in Czechoslovakia even one's body does not belong to oneself when the interests of the State are at stake. Anyway, Professor Reinberger 'agreed', and was quickly instructed in his new role, including the techniques of homosexual approach and seduction— the Czech Service has instructors for everything—while in London Major Jan Mrazek, the Intelligence man responsible for infil-trating the Labour and Conservative Parties, began to set the wheels in motion.

The Czech Ambassador invited Professor Reinberger to come to London to give a concert and naturally his old acquaintance Mr Heath was invited to the concert. A month later Reinberger went over again, and again Mr Heath was present at the recital. The two musicians soon got chatting and Mr Heath expressed his interest in one day playing the organ at the Church of St James in Prague, which is one of the finest 'classic' organs in Europe. Spontaneously Professor Reinberger said, 'Well why not come over and play it. Let me see what can be arranged.'

In my department we were overjoyed when Reinberger reported Mr Heath's request. It was exactly the opening we were looking for and we began setting the thing up at once. An official invitation was very soon on its way.

Several days passed. Then we received the answer we had been waiting for. Mr Heath had accepted! We were about to land the biggest fish ever caught by Czech Intelligence. If things worked out as we envisaged, we would have a leading British politician in our net, a man who would one day surely be a senior Minister.

Impatiently we waited for his arrival, but the future Prime Minister of Great Britain never came. At the last moment, some wise member of British Counter-Intelligence had warned the would-be organist that someone waiting for him in Prague was prepared to play another kind of tune. Thus the Heath Caper, which had taken two years to prepare, came to nothing.

In the autumn of 1961, when it seemed that I was not going to be exactly the star operator of my department, I had a wonderful stroke of luck. I found an agent who helped to destroy the value of Britain's whole strategic bomber offensive!

Marconi, as I code-named the young agent, was a naturalized British subject called Nicholas Praeger, whose father had been born a Czech. After long service with the British Embassy in Prague, where he had been an agent of Czech Intelligence for many years, the old man had retired to England, conferring upon his son the untold blessing of being allowed to live and work in a free country. And what had been young Nicholas's reaction to that great boon? Absolute contempt! He had spat on it, for Praeger was one of those young men—and there are many of them in the West—who are attracted to communism, not through their guts, but through their 'souls'. In the old days men became communists because they were hungry and oppressed; today, in the East, men join the Party because they are ambitious, want to get ahead, and know that the membership of the Party is essential to achieving that aim. In the West though, there are thousands of young fools—there is no other word—who are attracted for none of the above reasons. They are drawn to communism because of some romantic notion, a vision of Europe as it was in the days of Dickens which they want to put right with the aid of that heady faith from the other side of the Iron Curtain. But men haven't starved in Western Europe these thirty years and if there is injustice, one cannot even begin to compare it with the monstrous injustice reigning east of the Elbe.

Such a man was Nicholas Praeger, who was soon to fall into our clutches, where he was to develop from a silly young fool into an active traitor to the country which had adopted him and given him such a fair chance.

In 1959 he came on a visit to Czechoslovakia. We were waiting for him. We knew of his father's former activities and Praeger had made no secret of his communist leanings, although he was already working as an electrical engineer at the RAF Research and Development Institute! In Czechoslovakia, a man of that kind wouldn't have been given a job as gateman at Prague Airport!

One of our men, Lieutenant Husak (of whom more later), introduced him to his future wife, a Czech girl. She and Husak soon convinced Praeger of his true mission. He must become 'a warrior for the new world', actively preparing for that great day when his own country and the rest of the 'decadent West', which the Soviet Prime Minister had already threatened to bury, became part of the 'Socialist Brotherhood'. His head full of such notions, Praeger returned to England, soon to be followed by his wife-to-be, to become an active agent for Czech Intelligence!

Two years later I was handed Marconi, 'the radio man', as he was known within the Department. At that time he was of little importance. The stuff he was producing was of low quality and so I assigned him a low number on my own particular list of priorities. But in the autumn of 1961 all that changed.

At one of his routine meetings in London with his 'control', Bohumil Malek, he informed the Czech agent that he could sell him (in spite of his romantic notions of communism, he was not averse to money) the complete plans of a new anti-radar equipment which was being developed and tested at the place where he worked. This equipment would eventually be installed in Britain's 'V-Bomber Force', i.e. the Victor, Valiant and Vulcan bombers which formed, and still form, the basis for Britain's deterrent nuclear power. By means of this radar-jamming device, the bombers would be able to slip through the Russian radar screen and strike their targets. More important, for Britain that is, with such a weapon in its power, the country's defence against Russian attack was effectively secured; clearly the Soviet Union would think twice about launching its bombers and missiles against a country which could strike back so effectively. In short, the anti-radar device was the best defensive weapon and means of keeping the peace at Britain's disposal. This was what Praeger was now offering Malek.

But Praeger did not realize what kind of man he had to deal with. If he didn't appreciate capitalist society, Malek did! He knew he would have to return to the communist paradise later that year, but he wanted to postpone that departure as long as possible so that he could take more sterling with him to Czechoslovakia, where it was of tremendous value on the black market. If, however, he bought Praeger's device and the news got out, Malek would be likely to leave London at great speed. What was he to do?

Back at his office, he wrote out his standard report on what had happened at the meeting with Marconi. He wasn't pleased with the agent; in his opinion, the offer was a provocation on the part of MI5. The British counter-intelligence organization was out to compromise him so that they could expel him forthwith. His recommendation was—*don't buy*! My chief, Vaclav Taborsky, thought differently.

'So what,' he said, dropping the report on my desk. 'Even if they do expel Malek from Britain, he'll come to no harm. He's got diplomatic immunity. Order him to get on with it and write a recommendation on how the job should be carried out. And by the way,' he added, 'you're in charge of this one.'

We quickly arranged a dead-letter drop for Marconi, proposing that his film of the plans should be turned over in a foreign country, preferably France or West Germany. But almost as quickly we ran into difficulties. Marconi could not get the vital documents out of his institute to photograph them!

Naturally, we said that we would supply him with a German Minox to do the job within his place of work. But again that had a snag. Marconi would not be able to check whether the photos were correctly exposed or complete. And he couldn't keep photographing them until he was satisfied; that would soon lead to disaster. Ironically enough—and unfortunately for Britain's security—a new capitalist invention came to our aid just in time—the Polaroid camera, which had been introduced into the UK in 1961. Now Marconi would be able to check his photos in a matter of seconds. If they hadn't turned out as he had expected, he could take another. Of course, Malek at once emphasized the difficulties. Marconi would have to take a great deal of film into his place of work. What if he were searched? Besides there is a lot of waste from Polaroid film. Where could he safely dispose of it, and so on.

I overruled his objections and ordered him to buy Marconi a Polaroid at a well-known Oxford Street camera shop. At the next meeting with the traitor, he handed the camera over, showed him how to use it and, on my orders, told Marconi that he must carry it with him at all times. If he were ever quizzed by MI5 they would discover that he was a 'photo bug' who carried the Polaroid around with him wherever he went. Under no circumstances was he to attempt to conceal the camera, even at work. Praeger, eager for glory and an agreeable sum of money, began to snap the vital documents. The operation was under way.

Some time later I went on a courier run through Europe. After a week visiting agents on the Continent, I arrived in London to be met by a very agitated Malek. Hurrying me into his car, he took me on the tourist run round London before stopping by the fountains in Trafalgar Square. He parked the car and we pretended to admire the pigeons while he told me his fantastic story.

Two days before, Marconi had calmly walked into the Czech Embassy carrying a briefcase and asked for Malek. When Malek came in, he had handed him the briefcase and said baldly, 'They're in there'.

'What's in there?' Malek had asked, terrified by this major breach of security which could well mean an immediate end to his career in London.

'The pictures of the anti-radar device for the V-Force,' Marconi replied without a trace of emotion.

Apparently Praeger had become impatient with the slow-moving way in which socialist officialdom functioned. They hadn't found him a proper dead-letter drop; why not simply hand the documents over to our Intelligence himself?

I must admit that my own heart beat a little faster at that moment. Such stupidity could endanger the whole operation. But there was no time to worry about that now. 'Come on,' I said, 'let's have a look at the goodies he brought us.' The 'goodies' were perfect, almost too perfect, as I was soon to find out.

As a routine measure, our Prague-based Technical Division, which produced multiple copies of the report and photos, asked if I wanted one sent to Colonel Litvinov. After my Lonsdale failure, I thought it wouldn't do any harm to let him know that I'd brought off at least one successful mission, so I told the people from the Technical Division to let him have a copy.

A week later I received my first reaction to the Marconi photos. It came from the Czech Army General Staff. It was all very interesting, they wrote in their report, but, of course, their own Military Intelligence were well aware of the RAF project. It was nothing very world-shaking—just another jamming device.

Three weeks later the KGB evaluation came in. It really took my breath away. Normally the KGB always knew everything. It was standard operating procedure with the men in Moscow. 'Yes we know . . . already been solved . . . nothing very new, etc.' The Russians could never let anyone else do anything better or earlier than themselves. But this time everything was different. As far as I can recall it at this distance of time, the KGB report stated that Agent Marconi had turned over some exceptionally valuable information which had been adjudged by the Head-quarters of the Committee for the State Security of the Council of Ministers of the USSR (Russian titles always ran to lengths like that) as being the best information so far forwarded by our Czech friends. High praise indeed from our erstwhile Russian friends!

Further, the Soviet High Command confirmed that the information would be of the highest value in solving the air defence of Eastern Europe. While Malek should be reprimanded for the amateurish manner in which he had handled the operation, Agent Marconi should be highly rewarded and be informed that the USSR valued his information greatly.

Then came the rub. Agent Marconi would work forthwith under the direct control of the chief of my department so that there would be no further blunders and his findings would be reported to the KGB itself. Thus I lost my key agent, who continued to work for our Intelligence for a further decade, though he never again produced the kind of information he had supplied us with in London that day in 1961.

But that was not the last I was to hear of Marconi. When he was finally brought to justice after my defection, although I could not give evidence against him (it would have been classed as 'hearsay') I was told that he was no longer as cocky as he had been. Now he was pale and shaken. But I felt no pity for him. He had entered espionage knowing exactly what it was about. His overweening pride, his hatred of the capitalist system and his greed for money and good times had allowed him to betray the country which had adopted him and given him a good job— a job of trust—in spite of his foreign background.

THREE

The Czech Philby

In the spring of 1956, the Military Attaché at the Czech Embassy in London, Colonel Pribyl, received an amazing offer. In a typewritten letter—which was about the fifth copy, thus making it impossible for anyone wanting to trace the machine it had been written upon to do so—the anonymous correspondent offered his services to Czech Intelligence.

Such offers were nothing unusual to experienced attachés. What was interesting was that the unknown man offered to reveal the details of a large British-run spy network within Czechoslovakia—something the attaché had thought completely impossible.

But the attached memorandum soon shook Colonel Pribyl out of his fond illusions about the efficiency of Czech Counter-Intelligence. It concerned a Dr Potocek, a Director of the Prague-based First Czechoslovak Insurance Company, and showed that he was a British spy. There were no two ways about it. The anonymous correspondent gave a detailed account of his work for the British and *even included copies of the reports he had sent to his British case officer*!

The information filled Colonel Pribyl with alarm, for not only was Potocek a director of an insurance company, he was also an undercover Czech military-intelligence agent. If the information were true, it meant that our Military-Intelligence had been penetrated. Apparently Potocek, whose post often took him abroad, had passed British Intelligence the complete specifications of the then new T-54 tank, which was replacing the T-34 in the Red Army. Moreover, he had turned over samples of poison gases which were being experimentally manufactured for the Warsaw Pact armies. Concluding with the information that the Potocek Network consisted of eight paid agents and twelve unwitting ones, the unknown correspondent suggested that the Colonel verify the truth of his statements. If he were satisfied, he should forward his informant £1,000.

But Pribyl was another Malek. He did not want to rock the boat. He had a nice job in London, was saving plenty of money and was in no hurry to be expelled for espionage against his 'host country'. He decided that the offer was an MI5 provocation; he'd sit on it for a while and do nothing.

Unfortunately for the greatest spy network the world has ever seen, Pribyl did, however, mention the strange letter to a Major Louda, who was in charge of Czech State Security in London. Louda, a dedicated communist and always eager for glory, did not hesitate one moment. He dispatched a coded message to Prague straight away, asking for a check on Potocek and urgently requesting a contact man for the unknown correspondent.

A crash investigation was launched and in early September the first eight agents were arrested; two of them—Potocek and his closest collaborator, a technical translator—were sentenced to death. The others received long prison sentences. Among the unwitting agents was the Czech Deputy Minister of Finance, Jan Valek, who was a member of the Czech Central Commission for Party Control. The order went out—contact the unknown informant in London!

The clandestine meeting was arranged by Jan Mrazek, an experienced operator. Instead of the thousand pounds asked for in the original letter, Mrazek carried a bundle containing fifteen hundred pounds. Prague, usually so slow in these matters, had quickly realized that they had something really big on their hands this time. The unknown man did not introduce himself but got down to business straight away, while Mrazek sized him up.

'I'll pick the meeting places and times after this,' the stranger said in English. 'You're only risking expulsion. I'm risking my life.'

Mrazek did not like it, but the unknown man would have it no other way. 'I'm not risking my neck for anybody,' he said dogmatically. 'You must accept my terms.' Mrazek gave in.

'Good. Now where's the money?'

Mrazek realized at once what his new agent's motivating force was. He was not betraying men to their deaths in Czechoslovakia for ideological reasons; he was doing it simply for cash. As Mrazek handed the package over, the man stroked it with his right hand lovingly and muttered quietly, 'Just like manna from heaven.'

Thus agent 'Light' entered our lives. And he certainly deserved his cover-name, for he brought more light to bear on clandestine operations against Czechoslovakia than any other agent we ever had or were to have in the future. Thereafter the British desk in Prague became the most productive in the whole Intelligence organization. Even the KGB envied us our guiding light, if I may risk a pun, for it was a light which resulted in death for many Czechs.

Light was our Kim Philby, for not only did he enable us to wipe out a lethal network within Czechoslovakia, destroy a Czech resistance movement and effectively sabotage an anti-Czech organization located in neighbouring countries, such as West Germany, but through him we were able to arrange contacts for our own agents with every aspect of the British infrastructure. So much so that I can state categorically that I know of no other place in the world, outside of Austria and West Germany, where access to the Government apparatus, Parliament, the trade unions and scientific institutes was *at that time* so complete and on such a scale as in Great Britain.

The Light story began in 1948, when Light, whose real name was Charles Zbytek, was an honest citizen of the Czechoslovak Republic. In that year, a rather stiff and bad-tempered former Czech Army General Staff officer named Colonel Prochazka decided to take up arms against the communists who had just taken over power in his homeland and driven out a large number of officers such as himself. Opening an office in Hampstead, he started recruiting men with similar leanings into what he called the Czech Intelligence Office (CIO), with the active support of a certain Englishman who was a member of British Secret Intelligence (SIS).

With the aid of British money, the CIO spread right across the continent. It set up offices in Frankfurt, Munich, Zurich and Berlin, as well as in Austria and soon began to run its agents into Czechoslovakia to contact the surviving members of the national resistance movement and obtain information from them. Soon the CIO numbered nearly two hundred and had agents everywhere important. The whole new Czech communist infrastructure was penetrated by them.

In the early 'fifties the CIO received a new recruit—a handsome young singer from Moravia, who had been in England during the war with the Free Czech Army. During a visit to Wales as a member of a Moravian Choir, he decided to defect. Thus Charles Zbytek, then in his early thirties, entered the CIO group as a humble filing clerk, working directly for the bad-tempered Colonel Prochazka. Some of my colleagues maintained that it was Prochazka's rudeness and arrogance which caused Light to become an agent. I never accepted that explanation. I am sure that his sole motivation was money. Be that as it may, once Light had decided to spy for us, he was in an unrivalled position to supply us with the information we required. Although his job was poorly paid, it was, nevertheless, a job of no small responsibility within the CIO operation; for through his hands went the names of all the CIO agents. Light was slap in the centre of the action and he knew it. He grabbed with both hands and continued to grab, month after month for two whole years, at a cost to us of £40,000 in bribes and at a cost in human life and misery to the CIO which cannot be calculated.

By 1958 the CIO could only register failure after failure, which was hardly surprising with Light in their ranks. Eventually such financial support as they had was withdrawn and it became obvious that it would only be a matter of time before the CIO folded up. But that eventuality didn't worry Light particularly. He had already got a comfortable job running a boarding house in Folkestone and had sent his daughter to a Catholic private school, of all things!

Such was the situation when, in April, 1961, I became Light's case officer and began winding up the last of the cases that he had provided us with. And there were still plenty of them outstanding.

Most of the agents within Czechoslovakia had been eliminated (though not all, as we shall see). But there were still plenty of them in neighbouring countries who were highly dangerous to us. There was F. Urban, for instance, a nephew of President Novotny himself, and Jan Poula, the former Deputy Minister of Foreign Trade who, like Urban, was located in West Germany. In particular, I was worried by the activities of the Brussels office of the CIO, which covered the whole of the Benelux countries. This office was continually trying to subvert our foreign trade people visiting the Benelux on commercial missions.

Naturally Light had already given us the names and backgrounds of its leading organizers and agents, but still they kept popping up in the most surprising places.

There was, for instance, Engineer Adolf Cervinsky, employed in the commercial section of the Brussels Embassy. Cervinsky was a known quantity and a member of a long-time communist family. Indeed his brother-in-law was a departmental head in the Prague Central Committee of the Czech CP. During a visit to Brussels I contacted Cervinsky and asked him if he wouldn't like to begin working for us again in our operations against the local CIO and he agreed.

Some time later, back in Prague, I received an urgent call to come to the offices of the foreign trade organization, Centrotex, where someone was trying to poison a delegate from Brussels, a man named Cervinsky. Cervinsky was on the verge of a breakdown. He said that, as he left a lift, a man had stepped up to him and held a small bottle containing poison (or so he thought) in front of his nostrils. Just as he had been about to pass out, a woman had come up and his assailant had fled. I calmed him down and sent for a doctor, who confirmed what I had already guessed, that no attack had taken place and Cervinsky was in a state of nervous shock. I questioned him for a long time and finally he confessed that, in fact, he had been working for the CIO since 1948. The man I had set to spy on the CIO was a CIO spy himself!

FOUR

The Playboy Spy

One of the last important SIS agents in Czechoslovakia whom Light put the finger on was Mohamud Hamdi, the commercial counsellor at the Egyptian Embassy in Prague. Although he was pushing sixty, Hamdi remained the typical Egyptian lover; grey-haired and dark-skinned, he was a great man-about-town, always ready for another drink and another woman—and another adventure. For, in spite of the fact that his country was our ally and we were supplying its army with everything from tanks to our latest machine guns, Hamdi was a spy.

It was Light who first informed us of Hamdi's real mission in Prague. Apparently he was controlled from the SIS office in Vienna, his control being a certain Mrs Anna Mara.[1] Light (at that time still working in the CIO office) obtained his reports from Mrs Mara which indicated that it was Hamdi's job to supply the British with the details of Czech arms exports—a piece of knowledge vital to any assessment of possible war in the Middle East. Indeed, as Light found out, Hamdi's reports were thought so important in London that only three copies of the original (which Light had already seen) were prepared. Each copy was stamped TOP SECRET, SPECIAL IMPORTANCE (a classification similar to EYES ONLY).

Thus it was vital for us to put an end to Hamdi's activities. But how? We had no concrete evidence—only Light's suspicions. Besides, he was protected by his diplomatic immunity and was a representative of an Allied country. In the end it was decided to try to involve Hamdi in some sort of scandal which would force his own people to remove him. We would hit the playboy below the belt—where it hurt.

Hardly had we decided on this strategy when Hamdi actually

[1] Not her real name.

met one of his contacts in the open and was photographed passing a small envelope over to him in return for a larger one. Even the dummies of the surveillance team could work out what was happening. Then came the shock. When the photos were developed the contact turned out to be Senior Police Lieutenant Pavel Voda, a member of our equivalent of the CID. So Voda would have to be trapped too, using the same bait we had selected for the Egyptian diplomat—namely Venus.

Venus was a female agent who bore the unlikely name, for a Czech, of Gina Bianchi. In earlier years she had carried out a successful operation for us against an Italian who, in return for her exciting favours and statuesque figure, which had gained her her alias, had bequeathed her his name and a Tatraplan car, a very luxurious vehicle in those days. Thereafter the passionate Italian had been shown the door very smartly. But things had not gone too well with Venus. In addition to being a call girl, she had attempted to support herself as a singer in a Prague night spot. But her singing was so lousy that she was soon fired. Thus she had landed on our doorstep once more; and we hired her for the operation we had planned against Mohamud Hamdi. We did not realize what we were letting ourselves in for.

Venus was only too willing to get a job again, especially if it was on her back where she did not need to work too hard. An introduction was speedily arranged between herself and Hamdi. It was love at first sight. Money changed hands and Venus was on the couch, revealing her ample and highly exciting charms, in no time. The operation was under way.

Our next action was to introduce another female agent into the game; this was Gita, a blonde who had once held sway in the Egyptian's bedroom. In spite of her former membership of the 'horizontal guild', Gita was no fool. Speedily she worked out her own plan of how to involve Hamdi in a public scandal.

It worked like this. One evening Hamdi was entertaining Venus in the exclusive 'Olimpia Grill' (yes, there are such places in the classless society too)—champagne, soft music and even softer lights, the whole business—when who should enter, her pretty face flushed and angry, but Gita! Pushing past the waiters and striding purposefully through the crowded restaurant, she stopped in front of Hamdi's table. Alarm flashed across his face. Gita started screaming that he had been 'unfaithful' to her and was playing around with other women behind her back. Before Hamdi could stop her, she leaned forward and gave Venus a resounding slap. Venus was not the kind of girl to take that sort of thing lying down, although she took virtually everything else in that position. Shaking back her long hair, she jumped to her feet, upsetting the champagne glasses, and let Gita have a powerful right to the jaw! Suddenly everything was in an uproar. It was then that the waiting police, who just 'happened' to be outside, burst in and hurriedly ushered the two women to their car, leaving behind an unhappy and anxious Hamdi, who would not only be without a warm companion in bed that night, but who would undoubtedly have to face an unpleasant interview with the Ambassador the next morning.

The two call-girl/agents landed in the police cells that night, where they became acquainted with none other than Hamdi's contact, Senior Police Lieutenant Pavel Voda. Again it was love at first sight; for the gallant CID man invited Venus to share his own bed that night, instead of the hard bunk in the cell. Next morning a smiling Voda imposed a hundred-crown fine on the naughty ladies, paid, unknown to him, by their respective case officers, and they were let loose.

Now we could carry the tragi-comic operation a stage further. Venus was ordered to tell her ageing lover what had happened in jail—or *nearly everything*. The next night, she recounted her experiences with plenty of crocodile tears and sobs. It had been too terrible. The place was infested with bugs, was full of shocking people, whores, pimps and the like. Just too horrible to discuss. The only bright light in that ghastly place had been a certain Senior Police Lieutenant, who had attempted to cheer her up. Exactly how, she did not explain.

'Who was that?' Hamdi asked.

'An officer called Voda,' she replied.

We don't know what the Egyptian's reaction was to the news, but at all events he invited the 'nice policeman' to his home and the three of them, the two men who were unwittingly cuckolding each other and their big-bosomed mistress, took dinner together.

We were now ready to spring the trap which would safely see the CID man behind bars for his assumed treachery to his country and the Egyptian diplomat withdrawn from Czechoslovakia by his own authorities. But it was not to be. Somehow or other, the

SIS Office in Vienna had got wind of our little plot (perhaps they knew Venus was one of our agents) and ensured that Hamdi was withdrawn from Prague before we had time to set light to our fuse. Indirectly they did us a favour by getting rid of him, but still it hurt our professional pride to be deprived of our denouement—which would definitely have been a juicy one. Voda was dismissed the police, but turned up a little later in South America as a delegate of the Ministry of Foreign Trade!

The case of the Playboy Spy was the last major intelligence game in which Light was directly involved. By now the man whose file ran into thousands of pages was living a semi-retired life as a boarding-house keeper in Folkestone. He had changed his name to Charlie Charles and was doing little for us except recruit disgruntled members of the old CIO who were finding it hard to get jobs and came occasionally to visit their 'old pal'. They were easy meat for the arch-traitor and proved quite useful to our people working in the UK.

In 1962, Mrazek, who had first recruited Light, wrote and told me that he had died of a heart attack. Naturally he hadn't been there at the time, but he had reconstructed Light's dying hours from his daughter's account.

He ended his report with the number of Light's grave in Folkestone Cemetery (as was befitting in an official communication—one can never be too thorough) and the rather poetic comment on the arch-traitor: 'Here under this mountain of exposed agents and of unexploited opportunities lies the greatest agent of the Czechoslovak Intelligence Service. Amen!'[1]

[1] Even today I have my reservations about the manner of Light's death. Did he fall or was he pushed, as they used to say in the detective stories of my youth? He was a comparatively young man to die of a heart attack.

FIVE

The Department of Dirty Tricks

One of the ways in which our intelligence service contributed to the Warsaw Pact countries' propaganda war against the West was by disseminating false information (faked by ourselves) or deliberately creating provocative situations. Unlike the East, where no news can be revealed without the political censor's approval (in spite of the great fuss made about the dissident Soviet writers and artists, very few people know about them behind the Iron Curtain) the West leaves itself wide open to the Eastern countries' departments of dirty tricks.

The West's news media are only too eager to publish the 'dirt' about themselves, especially if it is presented in an effective manner—and our Soviet teachers were unsurpassed in the art of giving them the dirt. 'Bad news is good news,' they say in the media, and we were well trained by the KGB to ensure that the eager journalists on the other side of the Curtain were given plenty of bad news.

Thirty-seven-year-old Minister of the Interior Strougal, who took up his new job in 1962, was not brilliant, but he was well aware of the possibilities of the Department of Dirty Tricks. The young Minister was highly ambitious and soon realized that undercover operations which, by their nature, had to remain secret would bring him little fame. But propaganda coups, achieved by the intelligence service, could be broadcast to all four corners of the world and thereby increase his status and fame within the Party councils. Thus 1962 marked the start of important dirty trick operations from Prague.

One such operation run by the British desk, called 'Operation Wales', began when we heard that the Federal Republic of Germany was sending *Bundeswehr* panzer troops to practise at the British ranges at Castlemartin in Wales. Since its inception, we had

a

deliberately built up the *Bundeswehr* as the West's bogeyman—a collection of old *Wehrmacht* generals, only too eager to let loose another war against the peace-loving East in order to avenge their defeat by the Soviet Union in the Second World War. In fact we knew just how weak the *Bundeswehr* was. At that time we estimated we would be able to walk through it within forty-eight hours.

Still it didn't do any harm to keep Germany's new allies aware of the dangers inherent in a large German Army, officered by men who had once fought for Hitler. Operation Wales was born with that purpose in mind. It was short and sweet, but it achieved the maximum amount of publicity in the British press. Shortly after the *Bundeswehr* tank unit arrived at Castlemartin, graves were overturned at a nearby Jewish cemetery and swastikas painted all over them. Immediately the press got hold of the story. It was just up their street, especially those who were inclined to be anti-German anyway. The incident was splashed across the headlines of a lot of the cheaper British papers, with the innuendo that the *Bundeswehr* was strongly anti-semitic and was only waiting for the day when it could open up the concentration camps and begin warming the gas chambers again. Thereafter the young German conscripts, most of whom had been about two years old when the war ended, got a very chilly reception from the locals when they went off duty in the Castlemartin area.

Another dirty trick which we pulled at that time in the United Kingdom was directed against a nation of which we really were afraid—the United States. In 1962 a good number of scientists and technicians were leaving Europe for higher-paid jobs in the States. There, the universities, institutes and research organizations were crying out for 'brains'. Thus the idea of the 'brain drain' trick was born.

From London we heard from our long-time agent there, an MP known unofficially to us as 'Grandpa' or the 'greedy bastard' and officially as 'Lee', that one of his colleagues in the House of Commons was involved, on the side, in recruiting these scientists for a well-known American firm. We got on to it immediately. Lee was told to raise the matter in Parliament, with particular reference to the MP in question, who was somewhat of a thorn in our side. Thus we attempted to kill two birds with one stone.

The MP was discredited and Lee brought the whole business into the open.

The 'brain drain' concept provided an opportunity for those who didn't like the new 'Imperialists from over the Atlantic' to indulge in a great deal of vocal anti-Americanism. In my opinion it was one of our most successful coups and helped to sour Anglo-American relations permanently in intellectual circles within the United Kingdom. The 'parlour pinks' in universities throughout the country are probably still using the gimmick for their own purposes.

Of course, we didn't limit our dirty trick operations to Britain. No country in Western Europe was safe from us. For instance, we helped to manufacture the border conflict between Italy and Austria in the early 'sixties. This time our operation was much more dramatic and was borrowed straight from Heydrich's Operation Himmler of 1939, which had helped to precipitate the war between Germany and Poland. On that occasion Heydrich's thugs, under the command of Alfred Naujocks, who will go down in history as 'the man who started World War Two', attacked the German Radio station on the Polish-German border near Gleiwitz. The raid was made to appear as if it had been carried out by Polish irregulars. Next morning Hitler was thundering against the 'Polish bandits' who had carried out this 'dastardly provocation' and twenty-four hours later German troops were marching into Poland.

Of course, we didn't want to start a war, but we did want to cause ill-feeling between the Italians, who belonged to NATO, and the Austrians, who were neutral, but who could well be swayed into our camp, if they felt pressurized by the Italians. Accordingly we mobilized a large number of agents, not only in Austria but also in West Germany and Upper Italy, who carried out a series of bombings and destruction of power lines in the predominantly German-speaking rural areas of Upper Italy. (The territory had once been Austrian and the farmers of that part of Italy consider themselves Austrian and not Italian.) Leaflets followed, purporting to come from the Committee for the Liberation of the German-Speaking Citizens. Naturally the Committee only existed in the imagination of our Department of Dirty Tricks. Thereafter we withdrew from the area and let the hotheads on both sides get on with it, which they did with gusto! Almost immediately afterwards carabinieri started getting shot. The cold war on the Austro-Italian border, instigated by the Czechs, had become a hot war!

But, in the main, our dirty tricks were carried out against that nation which, on account of its recent past and the skeletons in the cupboards of many of its leading citizens, was most vulnerable —the Federal Republic of West Germany.

In 1960, one of our key agents in West Germany, Alfred Frenzel, a member of the German Bundestag and of that House's NATO Defence Committee, where he was privy to many NATO secrets, was arrested by the West German authorities. Frenzel, a Sudeten German from Czechoslovakia, had become an MP in Germany after his return to that country from England where he had served as a cook in the Free Czech Army during the war. Unfortunately he had allowed his wife to visit their homeland in 1956, where she had an illegitimate daughter. Naturally the visit came to the notice of our Intelligence and an approach was made to Frenzel. Money changed hands and Frenzel became our key agent within the German section of NATO, being run by the Major Molnar who had rescued my old friend Nemec from Austria. But in 1959 Molnar made a mistake. He decided that Frenzel, who was providing masses of information, needed a contact man to collect the stuff in Germany. *On twenty-two different occasions the contact man met Frenzel inside the Bundestag itself* before the German intelligence service became aware there was a top-level leak about NATO weaponry. Frenzel was investigated as a member of the NATO Committee and on 26 October a member of the BFV[1] spotted him passing information to his contact.

The loss of Frenzel's services, and the fact that General Gehlen's BND[2] had played an important part in his arrest by finding out that the Czechs possessed certain NATO secrets, determined us to play a 'dirty trick' on the General's organization.[3]

We had to wait until 1962, when our authorities agreed to allow

[1] *Bundesverfassungsschutz*—German counter-espionage.

[2] *Bundesnachrichtendienst*—West German Intelligence Service.

[3] We were not impressed one bit by the BND, in spite of General Gehlen's grandiose claims for his long-time spy organization. It had been thoroughly infiltrated by our men, as well as by the Russians. We even had an agent in the BND's HQ at Pullach.

a large number of Sudeten Germans to leave Czechoslovakia and go to West Germany. Immediately we went into action. Every single Sudeten German who applied for an exit visa was interviewed by our people. They didn't pull their punches. 'Listen,' they told the Germans, 'if you want to go back to your Homeland, you've got to sign this form saying that you will spy for us once you are settled in West Germany!'

Some refused point-blank, but most of them agreed to put their name at the bottom of the form. Of course the whole thing was a farce, because we knew quite well that they would go to the police the moment they arrived in West Germany, only too eager to report what the nasty Czechs had forced them to do.

It happened exactly as we had planned. The returnees reported in their scores to the BND men waiting for them in the Camp Friedland Reception Centre. The German intelligence officials were swamped by them. Reinforcements were rushed in, but they were still being swamped by the 'confessions'. Ordinary CID men were drafted in from Bonn to help out, but even then there were not enough officials to mop up this flood of revelations. According to our top-level source in the BND, the 'Czech Confessions' kept the rank-and-file of that organization busy for months! And of course, among all the bogus agents, we slipped in a good half dozen genuine ones, who were never discovered.

Another 'dirty trick' carried out against the Germans was 'played' the year after I had left for London, but it is worthy of mention because it illustrates Strougal's determination to get the maximum publicity out of Intelligence for himself and at the same time to hit the West Germans where it hurt most—in their National Socialist past. This was the Minister of the Interior's own brainchild—Operation Neptune.

Operation Neptune began in the middle of one night in the spring of 1965 when a little bunch of ragged civilians sank several mysterious chests in the twin Lakes Cerne (black) and Certovo (devil) in the mountainous area of Sumava close to the border with West Germany. Weeks passed. Then one day in May, 1965, a long column of trucks drove into the mountains towards the lakes. They were filled with security men and diving equipment. The security men were very reticent when the local villagers asked them what they were doing in this remote region. They mumbled something about 'Nazi treasure' and told the villagers to mind their own business.

A few days later the divers began their operations in the Cerne Jezero, the Black Lake, and sure enough they found several mysterious cases, which must have been there—so they told the villagers—since the end of the war. When the chests were forced open, they did not reveal glittering goblets or heaps of jewels stolen from some dispossessed Eastern European nobleman by greedy Nazis. Instead they were filled with mouldering documents written in German and bearing the legend *'Geheime Reichssache'*.[1] The chests were loaded on the trucks under the supervision of the security men and the party drove off. It should be mentioned here that the entire operation had been carefully filmed and recorded.

A few days later the bombshell struck the Western World. At an emergency press conference, summoned by Mr Strougal himself, the Minister revealed what the chests contained. A detailed account of Nazi operations in Central Europe! Confidently he read from the translations of a few selected documents, which showed that many people still prominent in West Germany were involved in wartime Nazi operations. West Germany, he emphasized, tapping the translations, was the legitimate heir to Nazi Germany and was run by the same men who had been active then. What was their aim? His answer was simple—to re-create the German Empire. In short West Germany was a canker on the body of Europe.[2]

The ambitious young Minister had created his sensation. Next day the world's press was full of the story, which read like some cheap thriller, complete with mysterious SS commandos and chests buried in remote mountain lakes. It certainly made Strougal known to the outside world and brought him to the attention not only of his superiors but also of those men in Moscow who in three years' time were to overrun my country. One wonders if they had already picked him then as a man after their own hearts: one who would be useful when the time came. Who knows? All I know is that today Strougal is the Prime Minister of Czechoslovakia, as is perhaps fitting for a man with such a twisted and

[1] Secret State Documents.
[2] For further details of this operation read L. Bittman, *The Deception Game*. Bittman, who defected just before I did, gives a full story of the operation, in which he actually participated.

62

opportunist mind. For it must by now be clear that the 'Nazi documents' found in the mysterious chests were mainly fakes. At the behest of the Minister most of them had been created by skilled forgers and German linguists in his own Ministry in Prague!

SIX

The Josten Operation

One of the last agents that I 'ran' during my stay in the British Department was a little ex-Social Democrat code-named Lev. Lev, whose real name was Jaroslav Hodac, had a totally different mission from all the other agents I managed in the United Kingdom. His job was to penetrate and report on the numerous exile Czech associations in London.

Prior to the communist take-over in 1948, Lev had been a member of one of the Social Democratic Party's regional committees. There he had been spotted by an agent of the CP, Dr Jan Nemec. Nemec, although posing as a Social Democrat, was in fact a communist who had been infiltrated into the SDP immediately after the war to spy on its activities. When the communists took over in February, 1948, they began to arrest the Social Democrat leaders, on the evidence turned in by Nemec. But in order not to compromise the latter, it was decided to find some 'fall guy' within the Social Democrats to allay any suspicion on their part that they had been betrayed by Nemec.

That fall guy was Lev, whom Nemec had rightly summed up as a very weak individual. Lev turned out to be an abject coward who would do anything to save his own skin. As it transpired the Social Democrats were arrested without incident and it was not necessary to use Lev. Nevertheless the story was given out that he had gone 'underground', which he had, but not in the way those Social Democrats who had managed to flee the country imagined. He had gone straight into a Security Service 'safe house' in the heart of Prague, where he started his training as an agent.

There the nervous little traitor learned all about secret inks, dead-letter drops, counter-surveillance and the rest of the tricks of the trade. A few months later, his training completed, he was dispatched to West Germany where he 'surfaced' again in a camp for political refugees.

In the camp, he carefully followed the instructions given to him in Prague by carrying on a large correspondence with the many Social Democrats whom he had known in the 'good old days' and who were now living in exile. The gist of all his letters was simply, 'Can't you get me out of this damned camp and let me get on with some useful work fighting those Communist bastards who have taken over our country?'

In the end his letters paid a dividend. His friends living in exile in London contacted some influential Labour officials on Lev's behalf. The Home Office was prepared to furnish the hapless exile with an entry visa and he finally landed in the arms of his fellow Social Democrats in London, who set to work to find him a job and a place to live.

One of them, a former Social-Democratic Deputy, Vaclav Holub, got in touch with one Josef Josten, whom he had known in the Czechoslovak Brigade on the Western Front, to enquire whether Hodac could fill the vacancy for a book-keeper's post at the FCI (Free Czech Information) News Agency, which was run by Josten and which also published the *Free Czechoslovak Weekly*. Holub explained to Josten that Hodac had had TB but that he was past the infectious stage and would certainly be a loyal and hard-working employee.

Thus Hodac found himself in a humble and low-paid job in Kensington, but he knew all too well that most of his income would be coming from other sources anyway.

While with the FCI, his job was purely clerical, though certainly of some importance to his Czech Intelligence chief, Lt-Colonel Vaclav Taborsky. He was now well placed to keep an eye on Josten, his new boss, who, of all the Czechs in exile, was probably most hated by the leaders of the Communist Party in Prague. At the same time, Hodac continued with his original task, to penetrate the Social-Democratic ranks in Britain, where he was absolutely trusted.

Little did I know that one day I myself would establish direct contact with Josten and provide him with a full account of what was going on behind his own back at the time. This is how it happened.

One day, in January, 1974, Josten read an interview with me in

The Times, and the paper almost dropped out of his hands when he saw what I had said: that he himself was 'twice set down for assassination, but these plans were called off . . .' He contacted me through my publisher and asked me for further details. I was able to send him a fairly detailed account of the Czech Intelligence operations directed against him personally and against his work—an ironic recognition of the journalistic and political effect of his efforts. This is, almost word for word, what my letter said:

'I have considered several times writing to you a few lines to tell you what I know about actions undertaken against you by the régime in Prague. This had to be delayed until the CIA in co-operation with MI5 unblocked part of the information which I gave them after my escape to the West.'

I then described my own career in the Czechoslovak Intelligence service and explained what had made me respond so readily to his request, namely, that I felt the world must be told what methods were being used by the Communist Intelligence Services, but especially

'to warn you to be more careful in your activities and during your day-to-day work. To be quite frank, I have never come across any one person as hateful as you in the eyes of the Prague Politburo . . .

'Now allow me to mention a few facts. After joining the "British Section" of our Intelligence Service, I read your file. It was of a remarkable size, it had thousands of pages of information about you and your activities, about your past, about your every step. Though Hodac was **sent** to London to penetrate the ranks of the Central Committee of the Social Democratic Party, a task in which he was exceptionally successful, after securing a job with you his duties were extended to follow your activities. Shortly after "settling" in London, Hodac came under the direction of Lt-Colonel Vaclav Taborsky—for about three months—and the rest of his stay was covered by Vice-Consul of the Czechoslovak Embassy, Major Bohuslav Malek. The Intelligence group was interested in your way of life, your financial situation, your friends, your family, relations, your state of health, your activities, FCI correspondents, etc.

'Reading your file, I was surprised at the force of hatred with which you were honoured by the leaders of the Republic, especially First Secretary (and President) Antonin Novotny, Secretary Jiri Hendrych, Vladimir Koutsky (member of the Party Secretariat) and Politburo member Zdenek Fierlinger (former PM and Speaker of the National Assembly). Through the intermediary of Rudolf Barak (Minister of the Interior) the "British Section" used to receive from the Politburo a deluge of various suggestions on how to thwart your activities, compromise you, and also, how to liquidate you.

'One of these campaigns followed a suggestion to falsify some of the materials of the (wartime) exile Ministry of National Defence from the years 1939–45. The falsified materials were to testify that you were "settled" in London (during the war) by the *Sicherheitsdienst* (Nazi Security Service). For this purpose, a pathetic disagreement you had during the war with General Neumann (CO Czechoslovak Forces) was to have been exploited. The background material was to have been "enriched" by evidence of suspicions that before your departure for exile you had had contacts with the SD . . .

'In 1957, the former Ambassador to London, Professor Dr Jiri Hajek, paid a visit to Prague and, on one of his walks, encountered in Republic Square a man who resembled you in appearance and gait. Dr Hajek wasted no time and called the Chief of the "British Section", Lt-Colonel Vlastimil Kroupa, and gave him the news. Kroupa informed the Chief of Intelligence and he in turn contacted Barak. Barak ordered an immediate alert of the "British Section" and of the border crossing points and border guards in the frontier regions with Federal Germany and Austria. Further, the patrols of Public Security Forces were strengthened. Your photograph was despatched to practically the entire Security Service in Czechoslovakia. But you seemed to have disappeared from the face of the earth. Though no one doubted Hajek's information, one obscure member of Intelligence, First Lieutenant Antonin Svoboda-Sochor, had some second thoughts. He knew the thick glasses of Dr Hajek too well, so he sent a cipher to London with a request to find out what Mr Josten was doing. The answer was, "He sits in his office in Holland Road and has not been away from London all this time."

'Further operations were not so innocent or humorous. On

the suggestion of Novotny, you were to be kidnapped. A special "diplomatic courier" was sent to London for the purpose—a technical officer of the 6th Directorate of State Security, who constructed on the spot a special box in which you were to be smuggled aboard a Czechoslovak State Airlines plane. For a long time afterwards, the box stood in the cellars of the Embassy building. Then, due to pressure of the "British Section" of Intelligence, the operation was abandoned. The "British Section", together with the "residents" in London, prepared a number of suggestions on how to carry out the kidnapping, but always added at the end their expression of disapproval because it could provoke undesirable reciprocal action and, consequently, endanger Operation "Light".

'Later again came from Mr Novotny the suggestion that you be assassinated. In your file I found a number of proposals, but one has to admit that, thanks to the "British Section", each of these ended with a clause making the whole project impracticable. One should also add that the chiefs of the Department at the time, were not at all happy about a scheme which tried to turn Intelligence work into butchery. They never agreed with such suggestions and always found ways to invalidate them.

'Besides these dangerous operations, you were subjected to some "jokes" by the London residents. Some were night telephone calls. As far as I know, these were made by Jan Mrazek and Major Jan Koska. Koska, a former Consul in London in the years 1962–67, was your "Guardian Angel" and devoted to you his untiring care. After his return to Prague, he worked in the 3rd Section of the 2nd Department of Administration B of the Chief Directorate of the Intelligence (SR). This 3rd Directorate was charged with counter-intelligence against British counter-intelligence, and worked to oppose the activities of the exile community in Great Britain. When Koska was in London, he had extensive contacts with our compatriots and some of these contacts included people who were your acquaintances . . . I am not free to give you their names. You have to be more careful in future. Anyhow, the above-mentioned group existed in London until my departure for the West, but it exists no longer. But that does not mean that the Prague Centre has been sleeping since 1969 and that a new set of agents is not now in operation. One cannot expect that people who have the blood of the 'fifties on their hands would hesitate before adding fresh blood to it.

'I wish you much success in your journalistic work and remain, with sincere greetings, Josef Frolik.'

However, to get back to the time in question, fate now took a hand and all plans for Josten's assassination had to be put to one side for the time being. One of our agents, who knew all about Lev's real role in London, defected. Hurriedly Malek, who was handling Lev, cabled us: 'Reserve a place for Lev in the Olsansky Cemetery.' We knew what that meant. Lev's cover had been blown and he had to be got out of London immediately! We wired Malek back that he should see that Lev left forthwith, but as he would be of no further use to us, he must steal all the files of the Czech Social Democrat Party in Exile and bring them with him.

This Lev did without too much difficulty, arriving later that night at Malek's quarters where he dumped all the records in the latter's car before hurrying to the airport where he flew to Switzerland for 'urgent treatment'. Thereafter Lev disappeared. Back in London, his alarmed 'comrades' notified the Swiss police. A search was carried out in the avalanche area of Switzerland. But no dead Lev was discovered under the snow, which wasn't surprising because Lev was already in Prague, comfortably installed in the Yalta Hotel, being prepared for his future debut on Czech Radio and TV when he was to reveal all about the 'machinations' of the Czechs in exile, working against their native country at the behest of the 'evil English cold war warriors'.

But before Lev could play his star role, we were informed that Zdenek Fierlinger, the chairman of the Czech National Assembly, had accepted an invitation by the British Labour Party to go to London and visit, among other things, the House of Commons.[1] The visit happened to be mentioned to Lev, who immediately informed us that once, at a meeting of the Czech Social Democratic Party in London, one of the committee, Blazej Vilim, former Secretary General of the Social Democratic Party, had announced angrily that he would consider it a great honour if he were granted

[1] Lev did eventually appear on television and duly delivered his hymn of hate against the British and their servile toadies, the exile Czechs. He is still alive and receives a Government pension of 1,800 crowns a month in recognition of his 'loyal' service.

the privilege of removing 'that dirty traitor Fierlinger' from the face of the earth.[1]

Lev's announcement caused some consternation within Intelligence circles. Immediately we informed Minister Strougal. His reaction was to postpone the Lev debut as too provocative and to inform Fierlinger as well as David, the Minister of Foreign Affairs.

David immediately saw the propaganda value in the affair. He called in Sir Cecil Parrott, then British Ambassador (today a professor at Lancaster University), and sharply pointed out that the 'revered' chairman of the National Assembly could not possibly accept the invitation to go to England because his life was actively threatened by Czech exiles, supported by British Intelligence. The Ambassador hurriedly assured the Foreign Minister that the matter would be taken care of at once; the visit could proceed as planned, and British security would take care of everything.

So Fierlinger was able to proceed on his visit and to find a few British politicians who were ready to wine and dine with a man who had been a secret Russian agent since 1937; who had worked within and betrayed the Czech Social Democratic Party prior to 1948 and who had helped the communists to power. Fierlinger is also a principal figure among the traitors who were instrumental in creating the situation which led to Jan Masaryk's tragic death.

But in spite of the combined efforts of the Czech and British security services, an incident occurred in London which destroyed the political purpose of the mission, for the information concerning which I am obliged to its instigator, Josef Josten. Josten found out that while in London, Fierlinger would be celebrating his seventieth birthday. He therefore sent Fierlinger a letter in which he said that it must be sad for him to be celebrating such an event away from his family, so he was sending him a memento to make him feel less homesick.

The gift was a small plexiglass paperweight in which was embedded a piece of barbed wire removed from what is known as the Iron Curtain. Copies of the letter together with replicas of the memento were sent to all the national papers. The paper-

---

[1] The threat had somehow been conveyed to the British police and a Special Branch officer had already cautioned Vilim. But we didn't know that at that time.

weight was shown on television and most newspapers devoted articles to it. Cassandra, the famous *Daily Mirror* columnist, described Fierlinger as a man 'who saw freedom die and helped to kill it'. A group of MPs, led by Sir Tufton Beamish, issued an appeal to their colleagues calling on them to abstain from any events connected with the visit. And many of them suddenly went absent.

Commenting on this visit and another by the present Czech Foreign Minister Jan Marko (in 1974), Bernard Levin wrote recently, 'I am well aware that in the modern world we (the British) cannot be too scrupulous about whom we talk to . . . There are times when democrats must sit down with tyrants and honest men with murderers; Churchill's famous precept—"jaw-jaw is better than war-war"—operates more powerfully and urgently than ever. But there is not the slightest necessity for any British Government to entertain officially, at any level above that of trade talks, representatives of the powerless and meaningless puppet government of Czechoslovakia, justly hated by its own people and rightly despised by Czechoslovakia's true rulers . . . shall we conceal that truth, or shall we promulgate it?'[1]

For me, however, the time had come to stop worrying about threats to kill Fierlinger or new plans to assassinate Josten. At the end of 1962 I was called into Taborsky's office, to be told: 'Josef, to make a good spy, you've got to have spent some time catching spies. You've put in that time now. You understand?'

I nodded. I was going to be sent on my first mission as a spy.

'Where?' I asked.

'London.'

[1] *The Times*, 12 November, 1974.

The Great Decision

In 1956, a Russian agent on his way back home in disgrace from the United States decided in one of his alcoholic moments—and they were many—that he had had enough of espionage. He staggered into the United States Embassy in Paris and demanded to see somebody in the CIA. He wanted to defect! Thus Reino Hayhanen, alias Eugene Nicolai Maki, indirectly entered my life, for I never actually met this man whose action that day was to have such a marked effect on my future.

The FBI checked the would-be defector carefully and decided that, although he was clearly unstable and an alcoholic, he was speaking the truth about the spy ring he had allegedly belonged to in the States. But apart from one sergeant in the US Army, whom he could identify, he knew practically nothing about the other members of the ring. In all his dealings with the mysterious spy-master, the latter had observed the strictest security precautions, except on one occasion when he had been forced to examine some material Hayhanen had brought him in his presence. He had taken Hayhanen to his storeroom, which was filled with photographic material. It was a start. But all that Hayhanen could tell the FBI men about the storeroom was that it was located somewhere in Brooklyn. The long search began until the storeroom was found, rented to a gentle, hook-nosed little man named Emil Goldfus. The FBI had discovered Russia's major post-war spy in the States, no less than Colonel Abel!

His trial began on 14 October, 1957, and was naturally followed with keen interest by all the Eastern countries' Intelligence services. In our Prague archive we had a large file on the subject, mainly composed of newspaper clippings and reports from our own people in New York, which I had read through several times in the late 'fifties. Then in 1961 a new piece of information was added to it: the details of a TV interview between the American commentator David Brinkley and Reino Hayhanen, suitably disguised with a wig and glasses. When I read Brinkley's final comment my heart started to beat a little faster. He said: 'That's the end of this spy story, but we are authorized to say, indeed asked to say, that if any others like Eugene Maki care to step forward any time, they will be guaranteed security, physical and financial.'

Those words were to become embedded in my mind, for it was clear from them that Brinkley was speaking for the CIA. In essence, he was stating that any spy who surrendered to the authorities would not be punished; indeed he would be rewarded and protected against the long arm of the Russian murder squads. It was the offer I had subconsciously been waiting for for a long time.

Ten years after I had joined the Intelligence Service, I was still hooked on the heady drug of espionage, but I had become sickened by the intrigue, the exploitation of the Czech masses, the office-seeking, the corruption of power—so much so that I was even prepared to forgo the drug. As I told my wife often enough in the early 'sixties when we were out walking in the country and couldn't be bugged, 'I cannot serve this régime much longer!'

Her only answer had been a troubled look, for she knew as well as I did the situation I was now in. I knew too much! I'd seen a lot, done a lot, heard a lot. Czech Intelligence would never release me now; as long as I remained in Czechoslovakia, my only way out of Intelligence would be feet first in a coffin. What was I to do? The Brinkley transcript had been a ray of hope on a black horizon; and now I was going to London. Little wheels had begun to click in my brain. Thus as I started my four-month training for my role as a spy in the British capital[1] a voice inside me told me that once I was safely established in London, together with my family, I was going to do what that Russian alcoholic had done—*I was going to defect.*

---

[1] It was the first real training I had received after over a decade in Intelligence—so much for the highly trained agents!

Target London (1964–1966)

'The trade of a spy is very fine, when the spy is working on his own account. Is it not, in fact, enjoying the excitements of a thief, while still retaining the character of an honest citizen? . . . the only excitement which can compare with it is that of the life of a gambler.'

Honoré de Balzac.

ONE

The Set-Up

On 21 April, 1964, I drove across Austria, Switzerland and France, arriving two days later in London, where I was given my official cover as Labour Attaché at the Czech Embassy. My career as a spy in a foreign capital had begun.

But first let me say a little about the Intelligence set-up in London at that time, which differs in hardly any way from the present situation there, and applied not only to the Czech Embassy, but to *all* the Eastern Europe embassies in London.

In those days we ran an 'Intelligence Collective', consisting of eighteen officers of State Security Intelligence and twelve officers of Military Intelligence, working under the cover of Embassy officials or employees of the CTK (Czech Press Agency), Cedok (Czech Travel Agency), the Czech Commercial Bank, etc. In other words, most of the diplomats at the Embassy were essentially spies, over whom the Ambassador, who was not a spy, was the official ruler—but in name only. The real power lay elsewhere, as I shall show in a moment.

It was the function of this Intelligence Collective to penetrate every aspect of the British infrastructure, in particular in the capital area to a radius of twenty-five miles, so that we could obtain intelligence about every sphere of the country's life. Thus when our Czech officials came over to negotiate a big trade deal with the British Government, our agent in the British Treasury could brief them every night on what the Treasury had decided on the basis of that day's talks, so that the following morning they could enter the conference room, knowing exactly what cards the British were going to play. Or when Kodak developed a new business technique which would prove very useful to our people back home, our agent neatly stole the machine in question and landed me, incidentally, with the awkward job of getting it out of

England. Three stout British Railway porters helped me to get it through the customs check for the paltry sum of twenty pounds. It was worth twenty thousand to our people—but that is another story.

So the job of our collective wasn't simply to obtain military information but also to get any kind of material, political, economic, social, etc, which could be used to help our nation and damage the one which was our host.

What kind of people made up this collective? Let me take the Ambassador, Dr Trhlik, first, although he was just a figurehead. Trhlik was a plotter and a pig, who continually tried to elbow his way closer to the trough, even if it cost the lives of others to do so. Today, after toadying abjectly to the Russian occupiers, Trhlik is Czechoslovak Ambassador in India.

The real head of our collective was Major Minx. He had as his deputy one of our Intelligence 'stars', John (Major Jan Mrazek, alias Ptacek), whom I have already mentioned, and who, in his turn, was supported by Captain Robert Husak, a handsome young playboy-gangster rather like the Russian Captain Ivanov of the Profumo Scandal; with one difference, 'Bob' was never caught.

The rest of my new 'comrades' were a strange bunch. There was Major Benes; officially he was vice-consul, but in reality he was one of us. He was an ardent socialist, blessed with a phenomenal memory and cursed with ragged nerves, which didn't help him much in his dealings with his superior, Major Jan Koska. Benes was a gorilla of a man. It was no problem for him, if he could not find a parking place at the Embassy, to lift up his British Ford by the bumper and turn it round. He was also a great drinker, who never appeared to get drunk, except for one time when Koska slipped a couple of knock-out drops into his whisky so that he could check his apartment out without interference. He got a surprise. *Benes was not only a member of Czech Intelligence, but also of the KGB!*

Another ugly giant of a man in the collective was Malek, who had handled the Marconi case for me. But, unlike Benes, he did not have one ounce of sense in his whole body. Once when a fly irritated him by buzzing around his office, he actually picked up a typewriter and flung it at the insect. I should imagine that his office held the Czech Service's record for damaged and smashed typewriters!

Malek was not the only 'dummy' among my new comrades. There was little Fremr, for example, whose brain had become addled by too much whisky. He was continually drunk and when he was, he was often seized by an unexpected aggressiveness, attacking his victim with the energy and dash of a terrier going for a bear. Once, in an advanced stage of intoxication, he lurched into Malek's office and told him: 'Comrade Malek, your behaviour here proves that you are a no-good villain!'

Malek flushed menacingly. He had had a bad day. He rose slowly to his feet and lifted the heavy table in front of him clean off the floor. 'Repeat that, you drunken slob!' he hissed. Fremr, fearless with drink, did so. Malek raised the table high above his head and let it drop with a thunderous crash that woke the secretaries out of their afternoon doze. Grabbing Fremr by the throat, he shoved him to the iron-grilled door with the words: 'You bastard, I'm now going to strain you through this door!'

He was only restrained when half-a-dozen of us piled on to him; otherwise Fremr might well have been picked up on the other side of the grille—in small pieces!

In short, they were a strange bunch, my new comrades. They included not only double-agents, lechers, drunks and crooks, but also former torturers and even murderers. Diplomats in name only, they went their various ways, joined only by the common bond of 'Intelligence', each seeking his own pleasures, protected by his privileged position and living as well as any member of the London jet-set on the money supplied by the hard-working man-in-the-street back in the 'People's Republic'.

Surveying them quietly in those first few weeks, I knew that I could not trust them; there would be no confidences here. But at the same time, I knew, too, that I did not have to fear them; they were too concerned with their own affairs. All, that is, save one man, Major Jan Koska, alias Klecka, the chief of counter-intelligence within the Embassy.

Koska was a big man in his late thirties who had been a heavy-weight boxing champion during the Nazi Occupation, which was evidenced by his pug nose. He had black, wavy hair and a pale oval face, which set off his dark, wary eyes that often reminded me of those of a snake. And in reality Koska was a snake—a reptile hated by every other member of the Intelligence Collective, for they knew that Koska's real job was to watch over them. He had to ensure that they did not deviate from the cause. Not that he took such things seriously himself. His major concern was to enjoy himself at the Czech people's expense and line his own pocket if he could.

Once I recall going with him and Husak to the La Campanina Club, where he threw money around as if it was going out of fashion. I didn't like it one bit. I thought, firstly, of the people back home sweating their guts out to pay for such extravagances and then of the reaction of the other guests. What must they think of communists like us, squandering money like water. 'Listen,' I told Koska in the end, 'I hope you've got the money to pay for all this, 'cause I haven't.' Koska looked across at me as if I had just landed from the moon. 'Josef,' he said drunkenly, 'don't worry about such trivia. The money will be arranged quicker than you can down that whisky. Let me see now.' He turned and began to look around the place. Finally he said, 'You see that dope sitting on the bar stool there?'

I nodded.

'Well, he's going to be our contact for this evening.'

'What do you mean—contact?' I asked, mystified.

He shook his head in wonder. 'Oh, come on Josef—wake up! An intelligence contact of course!'

Then I tumbled to it. Koska would write a report, saying he had made an interesting contact in the club and it had cost him so much money to make the man's acquaintance.

'That's right, Josef. He'll pay our bill for us and our working classes will thrill with pleasure at the honour of paying for this. Come on now, don't be a spoilsport. Let's have another drink.'

Thus I discovered that Koska, like little Fremr, was not averse to inventing agents and contacts in order to charge personal expenses to Intelligence Accounts. Later, for example, I heard that he had invented an English policeman who cost Prague £1,500 in bribes to cover Koska's drinking bills. When Prague wanted to know where to locate the man to turn him over to Koska's successor, the bobby had conveniently been posted to the Scilly Isles, where he could not be reached by Czech Intelligence. But Koska was no fool in spite of his crookedness. His superiors in Prague thought highly of him (as did his other masters, the KGB). Indeed, when Benes told the story about the invented policeman in Prague no one would believe him. Koska was an experienced, tough counter-intelligence man, one whom I would have to watch if I were to carry out my plan.

For me, I realized, in those first few weeks, Koska was the enemy, not the British MI5. I would have to be on my guard against him all the time. Once I dropped it, showed a weak spot, he would spring on me mercilessly and worry the truth out of me. How accurate my estimation was, I was to discover before my London tour was over.

TWO

Operation Shoe-Leather

In London that year I was once again a 'new boy'; and as is customary with 'new boys' I was given the dirty work. My assignment was to keep a check on an important NATO head-quarters in the Belgrave Square area. I was to try to find someone there who left himself open to blackmail or who might be bribed into working for Czech Intelligence and revealing the secrets of the establishment. It turned out to be the most boring job I had ever undertaken.

Privately I nicknamed it 'Operation Shoe-Leather', for in all my life I had never worn out so many pairs of shoes as I did on that job. Every afternoon at two o'clock I left our HQ in Kensington Palace Gardens, walked past the guards and started to run the gauntlet of MI5.

Naturally I knew that the Embassy was closely watched by British counter-intelligence agents. We had photographed them many times with our own cameras, so we knew the agents' faces as well as we knew our own. (The whole situation was quite ludicrous and one had to remind oneself frequently that this war in the shadows was being fought to the death.) Accordingly I took my time passing the MI5 hideout until my tail picked me up. Back in Prague they had already told me that the British service was so short of funds and men that it would be relatively easy to throw off their tails; they would only delegate a handful of men to such an unimportant person as myself.

That was easily said. In practice it was quite different. For the next three hours, I would track and back-track through Central London, taking taxis, tubes and buses in order to throw the MI5 men off. More than once, I would stop to ask strangers for a light, the time, the way—anything so that I would be seen in conversation with someone, because I knew one of my tails would then have to be detached to follow this possible 'contact'.

Finally, having lost my tails, I would arrive at my target worn-out, foot-sore and fed up. But my work had not yet begun. Standing outside the NATO HQ, in rain or shine, I would wait until some likely 'candidate' came out and then the whole business would start all over again. Sometimes the 'candidate' would go straight home, close his or her door and that would be that. Then I could limp home, take a hot bath and write up my negative report in peace. Unfortunately, the British, even civil servants, like their pubs and clubs; and so I was forced to track them from one hostelry to another until my head was buzzing with the noise, my bladder ready to burst with beer and my feet about to fall off. In the first month of my new assignment, I had worn out three pairs of shoes and my feet were covered in blisters.

Admittedly I did turn up a couple of likely possibilities. There was a one-armed civil servant, obviously a bachelor, who frequented homosexual bars. His name was passed on to our contact man (naturally I could not be endangered by doing the contacting myself). There was also a heavy drinker, who looked to me as if he might be in debt on account of his abnormal thirst. Again his name was forwarded to the unknown contacter.

The above might serve to show the layman that even in his own country, where naturally he has every right to think himself safe from a foreign intelligence service, his petty vices leave him open—if he is in any kind of 'sensitive position'—to the blackmail efforts of Eastern intelligence services.

After two months of this dreary, *hard* work, I was getting very sick of it. Surely there must be some other way of obtaining the information we needed from NATO Headquarters than this! I started to consider the possibilities open to me. Burglary was out of the question. The place was too well guarded and I had no idea of its internal lay-out. But if I couldn't get in, I reasoned, couldn't I get the information out.

It was then I had my brilliant idea. In the Shakespeare Pub in Westbourne Grove, I tried to strike up an acquaintance with the men and women employed in maintaining and cleaning the NATO HQ. In the main they were honest, decent working-class London folk. But one of them, an electrician called Tony (I never did learn his last name), did nibble. As it turned out he couldn't help me with the scheme that was beginning to form in my mind so I passed him on to Husak and started again.

I knew that secret material which had been dealt with was shredded inside the HQ (this was standard procedure), then taken outside to special trucks, which were waiting to remove the classified waste. There was no use trying to get the material between shredder and truck. That was out. Thereafter, the material was taken to the electric power plant at Putney, where it was thrown, bag and all, into the boilers. In other words, there was no check that the bag thrown into the fire really was full of classified material. Did my opening lie here?

It occurred to me that if (a) I could obtain bags similar to the Government ones and (b) find a willing tool in the power plant who would work for us, I could do a switch and no one would be the wiser. Then, with the classified material in my possession, it would be up to our experts in Prague (and we had experts for everything) to put the confused mass of shreds together again and make some sense of it. I put the idea to Husak, our tame playboy, already beginning the romance which, unknown to me, would make all my weeks of agonizing footwork useless. He approved it and we set about finding out what size and colour the bags in question were.

In the meantime we made a preliminary contact with the head of the trade union representing the workers at the Putney Power Plant. Under a pretext we visited Transport House, met the union official concerned and invited him and his fellow officials to a cocktail party we just 'happened' to be giving at the Embassy. He jumped at the chance, for it has always been my experience in England when dealing with trade union officials that the 'workers' representatives' like nothing better than to be entertained in the stiff, traditionally upper class surroundings of a London Embassy. Pleased with the way things were going, we returned immediately to Kensington Palace Gardens to ask the Ambassador's permission to put on a special cocktail party, aimed at getting our 'proletarian' guests in a receptive state for investigation. With a bit of luck we might find someone among them who could give us a lead.

But the cocktail party was not to be. A week or so before it was scheduled, Husak came swaggering into my office with a self-satisfied grin on his face, which usually indicated that he had 'scored', as he was wont to describe his amatory conquests: 'Well?' I asked.

'You can call off the op,' he announced, obviously very pleased with himself.

'Why?'

'Simple, Josef. I've already penetrated your target—and something else too,' he added crudely.

I gave a mock groan. 'Not another woman!'

'Yes, another dame—and she has access right at the top. Your days of beating the pavement are over, Josef.'

What had happened was that Husak had become acquainted with a German woman working as a top-level secretary at the NATO Headquarters, one, in addition, who was completely above suspicion because she was the niece of one of the most important, most powerful and most highly respected politicians in West Germany. With such a background, not only was she above suspicion, but nobody would ever dare make any serious investigation of her activities or her friends, however dubious.

Soon Husak was making love to her and obtaining classified information in return for his services. She was such a valuable contact that, two years later, Husak was requesting enough money from Prague to buy her a sports car. The accountants refused!

Thus my first little operation had come to a surprising and sudden end. After weeks of hard work, Husak had pulled it off in the comfort of a nice warm bed! Still, I didn't mind. My feet wouldn't have stood it much longer. But there and then I decided that there would be no more 'Operation Shoe-Leathers' for me. There must be easier ways of getting the information we needed than pounding the London streets for hours on end.

With that firm resolve in mind, I went to see the chief of the Intelligence Collective. After a few minutes of idle chatter—how was I getting on, was my wife settling down in the new environment, etc.—Minx asked: 'Well, Frolik, what's on your mind?' Briefly I filled him in on Operation Shoe-Leather and my attitude to it. He listened in silence, then said: 'Well, what do you suggest?'

I put forward my suggestion. 'Well I am the Labour Attaché here and since I've been at the Embassy, I've already made a lot of contacts with British trade union officials. Most of them are very sympathetic, especially the older ones because I think they still feel a bit guilty about the sell-out after Munich.'

Minx nodded his understanding. All of us knew that many

older Englishmen felt embarrassed in the presence of Czechs because, in a way, they blamed themselves (and rightly so in my humble opinion) for having sacrificed Czechoslovakia to Hitler in 1938–9. 'So?' my Chief queried.

'Well, with such contacts, why don't I try to penetrate the unions?'

THREE

Trade Union Brethren

I have said earlier in the book that the libel laws of Great Britain act as a more powerful form of censorship than any bureaucratic blue pencil wielded behind the Iron Curtain. For this reason it was thought advisable that the following chapter should be dropped. I argued that the names themselves were of marginal importance and thus a number have been deleted. My intention was not, by any means, to raise doubts about the loyalty to their country of individual members of the British Trade Union organization but to show the lengths to which 'diplomats' accredited to the London Embassies of the Eastern Bloc will go in their efforts to 'cultivate' important Trade Union officials. I must emphasize that, although I was repeatedly warned off for trespassing on Russian territory, I have no evidence that the Russians succeeded in their aims. Nevertheless, the fact remains that Trade Union officials were, and still are, prime targets for communist agents in Great Britain.

The British Communist Party,[1] as we all knew in the Embassy, was a downright failure. After half a century of really hard work in the United Kingdom, it had never had a membership larger than—say—sixty thousand; and at general elections it had never polled more than one hundred thousand votes. The number of MPs it has had in Parliament can be counted on the fingers of one hand. Yet, in one particular field, it has shown outstanding results, in relation to its exceedingly small numbers—the trade union organizations.

[1] Incidentally, we were not allowed to recruit members of the British CP. It was expressly forbidden by Prague.

By virtue of a great deal of hard work and the intensive training of the communist organizers in the union movement, most of whom leave the normal non-communist union leader standing when it comes to any kind of debate or discussion, and sheer twenty-four-hour devotion to the job in hand, communists had begun to penetrate union leadership very effectively by the early 'sixties. So much so that today communists control over 10 per cent of the important posts in the major unions: a figure ludicrously out of proportion to their actual numbers. Thus communists virtually control the Scottish and Welsh (and probably the Yorkshire) sections of the National Union of Mineworkers; are especially strong in the Amalgamated Engineering Union, with 27 communists or 'Marxists' in its 52-strong national committee; and have an important say in the affairs of the giant Transport and General Workers' Union.

And the communist trade unionists make little attempt (especially those at the lower level) to hide their sympathies. In January of 1974, for example, that veteran communist, one-time miner Idris Cox, who has been the secretary of the CP's International Department since the 'thirties, stated publicly at a party meeting: 'Our comrades hold key positions in influential organizations at a regional and national level and the stand of some of the unions on fundamental issues is shaped under their influence.'[1]

But it took Mr Bert Ramelson, the Ukrainian-born Industrial Organizer of the British Communist Party, to reveal the real significance of the communist infiltration of the unions, when he boasted that the CP only had to 'float an idea early in the year and it can become official Labour policy by the autumn'.

Why? Because if the communists can dominate the unions, they can also dominate the Labour Party. Thus the two big unions, the Transport and General Workers, and the Amalgamated Engineering Union between them can play a decisive role at any Labour Party autumn conference *where they control no less than forty per cent of the vote!*

Naturally, we were already aware of the trend within the unions way back in the mid-sixties; and our people in London actively encouraged the contacts between the TUC and officials of the communist-controlled World Federation of Trade Unions.

[1] *Daily Telegraph*, 28 January, 1974

As I write these very lines, we are informed by the press that secret talks have been going on between the TUC and the WFTU, and that a delegation of key union leaders is to tour Hungary and Czechoslovakia, perhaps as a follow-up to those talks.

And who arranged the key talks? No other than two former colleagues of mine, Mr S. Ulik and Mr Josef Lebl, respectively Second and Third Secretaries at the Czech Embassy in London—*officially*! Unofficially they were something else, as the British Government's expulsion of them earlier in the year shows; they were both accused of spying!

But to return to 1963. By that time, I had been in London nearly a year and in spite of my only average English, I was, I think, a welcome guest at TUC parties and receptions and in the private homes of some trade union leaders. With most of them I was on a first name basis—they had downgraded my Czech Christian name to the chummy English 'Joe'—and some of them even came to my own home for food and drinks, especially drinks!

There was —— of the —— Union, whom I first met at the TUC Conference in Brighton. We were soon firm friends and I was often invited to his home, where I met his wife. She herself was a communist, as was her husband, though he kept his Party membership secret. Why? I can only conjecture that a notorious friend of the family had something to do with it. He was none other than Lieutenant-Colonel Nikolai Berdenikov, whose name first attracted attention in connection with the Penkovsky affair.

I had first met the charming Russian Colonel, who, like myself, was an Intelligence officer with a diplomatic cover, at the Brighton TUC Conference in 1965, where I was seated at a table with Ted Hill, Harry Nicholls, the General Secretary of the Transport and General Workers' Union, and Mr Callaghan. After the dance that night, Berdenikov, who officially was Soviet Labour Attaché, returned with me to my hotel near the front. Naturally he knew what my real job was in England, just as I knew his. We chatted about general Intelligence matters for a little while; then I remarked that we were missing a great opportunity for Intelligence by not using the Irish Nationalist Movement, the IRA. Berdenikov laughed and promptly proceeded to fill me in. In 1945 the NKVD had seized all the *Abwehr* files in Berlin, including those concerned with the *Abwehr* apparat within the

IRA during the war. The *Abwehr* was the German Intelligence Service, which regularly ran agents into Ireland during the war, although they were never very successful because their IRA collaborators were usually more interested in the money they brought with them (and the resultant drinking parties) than in carrying out espionage missions. Boastfully he said, 'We won most of their people over to our side and we could unleash a national liberation struggle against the British at any time. We would consider ourselves fortunate if we had a network similar to the one we have in Ireland here in England.' At the time I thought he had drunk too much Scotch. Today's headlines make me think differently.

This, then, was the man who was a frequent guest at the —— home, a powerful man who jealously protected his own contacts and agents; for when I asked Prague for permission to recruit —— for Intelligence purposes, I received a very smart reply: 'Hands off! That particular mare is being run from another stable close by.'

One didn't need to be clairvoyant to realize where that stable was and who was running the mare. The owner of the stable was undoubtedly Colonel Berdenikov. A little while later I ran into a similar stumbling block when I started to cultivate the friendship of Union Leader ——. Husak arranged a couple of cocktail parties for him at the Czech Embassy; later I invited him to my flat at 34 Bayswater Road (incidentally the wartime home of the exile Czech Intelligence Service, the forerunner of my own).

——, then in his mid-fifties, turned out to be a friendly, sociable man, with whom, I like to think, I got on very well. I started to cultivate him. But such things cost money. My expenses started to mount. They were forwarded to Prague, from whence, a little later, I got the brisk order: 'Drop the —— project. He's a horse of friends!' Again, unwittingly, I had bumped into one of the Russian Colonel's contacts, if that's the right word for it.

Then I thought I had struck lucky at last. At an Embassy Party for British trade union leaders, I was introduced to —— of the —— Union. The party was nearly over, but I, and —— still thought the night was young. Accordingly I invited him back to my place for another drink. One drink developed into several and soon we were on a first name basis. Just before he departed, I pulled a bottle of brandy out of a cupboard and handed it to him. He looked so poorly dressed that I thought I was doing him a favour by giving him the drink; after all drink prices were pretty high in England in those days and he seemed a nice enough chap. A little surprised, he accepted it and went on his way. That, I thought, was that.

Three weeks later I received a pleasant surprise. —— invited me to come to a party at his house. But I received an even greater surprise when I arrived. It was a real villa of the type once owned by the richer classes in my own country. And this place belonged to the man to whom I had so generously given one lousy bottle of cognac! Even today I blush at the thought of what a fool I made of myself.

The evening passed pleasantly enough. The ——s showed some slides they had made of their travels in Eastern Europe and asked me to give a brief commentary on them on behalf of their guests, some twenty or thirty people. I did my best, then sat down again to enjoy a few drinks with my host.

Suddenly, completely out of the blue, he asked: 'Where's Nicolai?'

I knew that he must be referring to my Russian rival and mentioned that I happened to know that Berdenikov was out of town that night. —— nodded and dropped the subject immediately, leaving me puzzled by what his connection was with the Russian agent. A little while later Berdenikov answered my question himself. 'Joe', he said. 'Keep your hands off ——. You can visit him socially, but that's all. You understand?' I understood.

But I continued to visit ——. Our families got on well together, he was a nice chap and good company; and besides nobody had ordered me not to continue seeing him. So I kept up the visits. Thus it happened one night, when we had had a lot to drink and the rest of the company had left, that he took me to one side and said quietly, 'Joe, I know you're disappointed in me.' 'What do you mean?' I asked. He winked knowingly. 'You know and I know, Joe. I've realized what you were here for from the very start.'

I tried to protest, but he held up his hand for me to be silent. 'Now don't try to lie, Joe. Besides it doesn't matter. I can be of no use to you personally. But I have a good friend, who might well be. At the next most convenient occasion I shall introduce you to him.'

Thus, leaving me suitably mystified, he dropped the subject and we concentrated on the more satisfying business of emptying a bottle of Scotch together.

For several weeks nothing happened. I started to concentrate my attention on another trade union official who we were attempting to recruit. He would have been a prime catch for us because his union indirectly controlled the publishing industry in the United Kingdom. If they wished they could stop the publication of most of the books and all the newspapers in the country. If we could recruit the man it would give us a tremendous weapon in time of crisis. Imagine if, on the outbreak of a war, the enemy could paralyse the whole supply of printed information in the United Kingdom. Later when I tried to check his file in Prague, it had vanished. I knew what that meant. The Russians had taken him over; he was too important for the Czechs.

Then I was invited to a really big party by my friend ——. During the course of it, —— asked me to go and wait in an ante-room. A few minutes later he returned. 'Joe, you remember the friend I told you about?' I nodded. 'Well, here he is. May I introduce ——?' I took the other man's hand. '——?' I queried, for I had never seen the stranger before at the other union functions I had attended. Later I was to become more than familiar with his face through his frequent appearances on TV.

But I was not destined to take the matter any further, for a few weeks later I received a very strongly worded order directly from the Prague Ministry. In essence, it said: 'Keep your nose out of the British trade unions. They are none of your concern. Your business is with NATO.'

But I had no time then to consider the reason why Prague had suddenly decided that I should have nothing to do with the Unions. There were too many other operations going on which took up my time—and, in addition, the suspicion was beginning to grow within me that I was being shadowed.

FOUR

Lee, Gustav and Others

In the mid-sixties, Czech Intelligence in London was running thirty full agents and a couple of hundred contacts of various degrees of importance. We had our agents in Parliament, the Cabinet, the Trade Unions, the Police, the Treasury, Government Research, private business, etc. Just eighteen State Security Intelligence officers running all those agents—that was over twenty agents per officer, which is a lot for one man to handle.

How had we done it? After all we were one of the smallest countries in the Warsaw Pact group. How had we achieved such tremendous results? As I have already said, British Security was fairly lax, not because MI5 was incompetent—it is highly rated in the East—but because it was undermanned and underfunded. In years to come its Deputy Head was to say to me: 'Joe, you have done this service a great favour. Your revelations have finally made our authorities aware just what is going on in London. Money is beginning to flow into our office at last.' With so few resources at its disposal, MI5 concentrated on the representatives of those countries which they really thought were dangerous, namely Russia and Red China, and naturally we profited from this allocation.

But that wasn't the only explanation of our success in those years. Another reason was that all our operatives were highly trained. Most of the officers in the collective had been in Intelligence for nearly twenty years, some of them having joined as early as 1945. Indeed I was very much the 'greenhorn', with my ten years of experience. We knew all the techniques of subversion—indeed, most of us had served in counter-intelligence at one time or another and had seen the same techniques applied against our fellow countrymen by the British and Americans (something which was quite new to our Russian colleagues, whose country was too remote to have been subjected to such things). And in the final analysis, we had money—plenty of it! Money, which in the end, buys everything and everybody!

In September, 1974, the following appeared in *Private Eye*: 'Delicacy and good taste prevent me from mentioning the names of two Labour MPs who are at present under investigation by the Special Branch for their connections with an Eastern European embassy. However, I should point out that the Czech Embassy, which covers espionage and dirty tricks for the whole Soviet bloc, allocates £20,000 a month for "gifts", "retainers" and "consultancies" to politicians, journalists, civil servants and others who might prove useful.'

Readers may be interested to learn how such money is raised. At a time when luxuries such as chocolate, tea, coffee, nylon stockings, razor blades, even cars, were either unobtainable or so expensive as to be beyond the means of ordinary people, the Czech Government imposed a prohibitive import duty on all gift parcels, e.g.: £3.10s., as it then was, on a pound of tea or coffee. At the same time the so-called Tuzex coupons were introduced (which are still in use), obtainable in London or Chicago from Czech Government representatives or from local agents. These were exchanged in Prague on a 5:1 ratio to the normal currency, or they could be used in special government stores which sold goods either for foreign currency or for Tuzex coupons. There, all these luxuries were in ample supply. This led to the development of an incredible black market for the coupons, but the Government did not mind. In one year, it collected twenty million dollars in the US and Canada, and hundreds of thousands of pounds sterling or other hard currency, which remained at the disposal of the Czechoslovak 'missions' abroad.

Needless to say, those of us who knew the real purpose of this scheme could not understand why it was (and continues to be) tolerated by all the Western Governments. Just open any exile paper in the US or Canada and you will find it full of Tuzex advertisements.

Let me now explain how the money was used. Take the case of a journalist. One day he is approached by the Czech Intelligence Agent, who begins his ploy something like this. 'Listen, old chap, back home they're having a hell of a time with the potato harvest. They must be planting the wrong kind or something. The harvest this year is going to be the worst for decades.'

94

Journalist: You don't say! Our farmers are doing OK, according to all accounts.

Czech Intelligence Officer: Naturally, because you're using the right kind of potato for the soil. Those buggers back in Czechoslovakia are only going to plant communist potatoes, even if they grow to be no bigger than a canary's balls. But you could do me a great favour. I mean potatoes are highly important for our economy. Those sods back in Prague won't listen to me, but they would to you!

Journalist: What do you mean?

CIO: Well, if you wrote an objective report on the state of British potato farming, they might get it into their thick communist heads that a new type of potato could be a boon to Czech agriculture. But I wouldn't expect you to do it for nothing. I'd have to indent for expenses of course. But you'd be paid.

Journalist: Well, I'd certainly like to help if I can. I'll see what I can do.

Thus the story is written and handed over by the journalist, who receives a handsome retainer for his 'contribution to Czech agriculture'—after signing for his fee. As soon as he has gone, the 'vital report', which will 'undoubtedly have an important bearing on future Czech potato farming', is torn up and thrown into the waste-paper basket, but the journalist's receipt is carefully filed away in the Intelligence man's safe, the first of many such receipts.

A few months later the crunch comes. The journalist is invited to come and see the Intelligence man. But now his old pal has changed; he is all officialdom. The days of the potato report are over. Now the once friendly Czech wants to know the extent of the new runway at Upper Heyford or whether the XX US Air Force Reconnaissance Squadron has really left Mildenhall for Spangdahlem Air Base in Germany, or whether it has been moved to Madrid-Torrejon.

The journalist is shocked. 'But that's military information,' he stutters. 'I can't do anything like that!'

The Czech Intelligence Officer is polite but firm. 'Naturally you can.'

'You can't make me. I'll go to the Police.'

The moment of truth has arrived. A little walk to the safe, the pile of receipts is dropped casually on to the table of the journalist and the Czech says: 'And what do you think the Police will say about these?'

The journalist takes the morning train from London to Oxford. The length of the new runway at Upper Heyford will soon be worked out.

With British MPs we had another standard procedure. (All these approaches are taught at the Intelligence School in Prague.) Instead of the situation of the British potato *vis-à-vis* its Czech counterpart it would be Anglo-Czech relationships. At a party the target MP would be regaled with plenty of drink and the conversation carefully steered around to the situation existing between the two countries. 'What a shame that one cannot do something about improving the relationship between ourselves and your country, sir,' the Czech Intelligence man would remark, looking sorrowfully into his glass, filled with well-diluted Scotch, unlike that of his British counterpart. 'How do you mean?'

'Well, you must realize how suspicious our people back home in Prague are of British intentions. After all you are a member of NATO and all that—and in Prague one is so isolated. I mean they don't know the British like we do here in the Embassy. What really fine people you are, if I may be so bold. Another drink?'

'Thank you. You really think that your people mistrust our intentions?'

'Yes, I doubt if most of the powers-that-be in Prague have really realized that the Cold War is long over as far as the British are concerned. If only we could find *someone* here who could convince our people—even in writing—that the British are only too eager to improve their relationships with their old wartime allies!'

Naturally the penny drops. A report is written. Money changes hands. 'Of course, we couldn't allow you to write all this for nothing, sir!' Other reports follow and our MP is trapped. Soon he is in the same situation as the journalist. Almost without noticing it, our MP is now an agent of the Czech Intelligence Service.

Naturally, these relatively subtle approaches were completely wasted on some of our agents in London. All they were concerned with was money. 'You hand over the cash and I'll betray my country.' In other words, a simple business deal, information for pounds sterling. 'Lee' was one such agent.

'Lee' was a Labour Member of Parliament who had been recruited for Czech Intelligence in the mid-'fifties by Lt-Colonel Jan Paclik (alias Novak), then the Second Secretary at the Embassy. Although 'Lee' was only a rank-and-file MP, he had managed as a back-bencher to get himself a position on the Committee on Defence, which put him in a unique position to hand over military information to us. Once when I was in the Embassy's safe room—the safe room, a feature of all embassies, is a room built within a room, which is completely proof against any kind of bugging, however sophisticated. It is here that all Intelligence meetings are held—I saw top-secret material of the highest military value which he had delivered to his handling officer. It concerned the British Army of the Rhine, Britain's contribution to NATO, the Russians' and our number one priority.

'Lee' was interested solely in the five hundred pounds a month retainer which we gave him. He had no ideological reason for spying for us. All he was concerned with was hard cash and anything else he could pick up which might feather his nest. In spite of the obvious danger, he was always demanding free holidays in Czechoslovakia so that he might save the expense of having to pay for his vacation himself. He even went as far as pocketing as many cigars as possible whenever he came to the Embassy for a party. Thus for nearly fifteen years the little miser met his handling officer once a week while he was taking his dog for an early morning stroll in a London park near his home and passed over information of the highest importance.

Another MP bought for money was 'Gustav', recruited by my old chief, Taborsky while he was in the London Embassy in the mid-'fifties. 'Gustav' was not as important as 'Lee', but he was in a position to deliver interesting information about the domestic and foreign policies of the Labour Party while it was in opposition, and later, when the Wilson Government came to power, about defence matters.

But these two MPs pale into insignificance in comparison with the catch we made in the late 'fifties. This time both money and sex were involved. The man in question was an MP who had been involved in some sort of homosexual trap in Czechoslovakia. Not only was he blackmailed, but also given a sum of money for his services to Czech Intelligence. Fortunately he was given an interesting job in the Wilson Government in 1964, and although it was not of Cabinet rank, it did put us in a position to know a great deal about certain British military and counter-intelligence operations. Again money changed hands and a fresh traitor appeared among those men who had been selected as honest, decent, responsible men to represent their fellow citizens at Westminster.

Sad to say, six years later, when I came to give evidence against these traitors, it could only be classed as hearsay and all three were freed. Although the Member in question was never brought to trial and Mr Wilson reportedly nearly 'hit the roof' when he heard of his treachery and dismissed him forthwith, I saw in the recent [October, 1974] British election results that he is still in Parliament as a back-bencher. What a mockery such men make of democracy!

Naturally there were people in England who wanted to work for us for ideological reasons—convinced communists who felt that the British system was rotten and should be torn down, regardless of the methods used. We accepted their offers gratefully. All the same, working on the precept that had been drummed into us in Prague, that a friend can drop out of the business any day, a *paid* agent never, we ensured they received money from us and *signed* for it. Be it in the form of a Christmas gift or a birthday present, sooner or later they accepted money from us and thus became paid agents who could never go back.

Bernard Levin, writing in *The Times*, under the apt title 'Pulling Strings for the Czech Puppets', points out that there are still plenty of 'parliamentary freeloaders, who want nothing to interfere with their hopes of sipping Czech beer next summer in a café on the banks of the Vltava'. Little do those 'parliamentary freeloaders' realize how open they are leaving themselves to being bribed or blackmailed into working for the Czech Intelligence Service!

May I, as a long-time agent of Czech Intelligence, who in the years of my service have, sadly, subverted enough people of all nationalities, offer a few words of warning to all who read these lines? Under *no* circumstances accept money from any representative of an Eastern Embassy or official organization! Back in Prague, for instance, our accountants are as strict as any employed in a large capitalist company. Everything must be accounted for and they tolerate no gifts or money, unless they serve the purpose of obtaining information (although skilled operators like Koska could always cook the books). There are no such things as 'gifts', 'retainers' and 'consultancies' in the Czech service or in that of any other Eastern Intelligence Department—there are only *bribes*!

FIVE

The Trap

During my time in London, I had never taken any security precautions as far as my flat in the Bayswater Road was concerned. All the secret material I was currently handling would be left in the safe at the Embassy; therefore there was no need for me to secure my flat against unwelcome visitors.

Naturally I knew that MI5 made regular checks on the apartments of foreign diplomats from the Eastern European countries. As far as I was concerned, they were welcome to search my place at any time. Whenever we went away for a weekend, I always left my flat keys with the porter, instructing him to make use of them if there were a burst waterpipe or a gas leak. Nor did I attempt to play tricks with any would-be searchers, like placing a hair between a lid and a drawer, or by measuring the exact position of some object.

But in mid-1965 I realized that my flat was being 'visited' in my absence. Naturally it had been 'visited' before—by MI5. Now, however, the visits were pretty obvious. There would be a cracked vase or overturned lamp, or a bottle of whisky or cognac would have vanished mysteriously: something the trained men of British Intelligence would never have done. Gradually I began to realize that the unknown investigators did not come from 'the other side', but *from my own team*!

Indeed I was sure I could pinpoint the man in question. Just prior to the start of these searches, one of my colleagues had moved into my neighbourhood. In itself that was nothing very strange. But this man worked directly for the hated Major Koska. His name was Major Vilem Moravec, the Embassy's radio man. Normally it was his job to check the Embassy out at regular intervals to ascertain whether or not the place had been bugged again by the British. Otherwise he was engaged in recording the communications of the British Surveillance Team, set to watch the Embassy, and send his results to Prague where our experts tried—often in vain—to unscramble the tapes.

Moravec was not very busy by comparison with me and my colleagues who were running so many agents and contacts. He had plenty of time on his hands and presumably Koska had decided he was the man to carry out the operation against me. But why? That was the problem that engaged my mind during the summer of 1965. Was Koska carrying out a routine check? Or was there something more to it? Did they already suspect me? Had they guessed that I was planning to defect? Did it show that clearly? A hundred questions, in short, but damned few answers!

In September I decided to invite my mother to come and visit us for Christmas. This might be the last opportunity we would have of seeing her for many years. As soon as I defected, I knew that I would have to cut off all contact with my family. The British authorities gave no trouble. The Home Office quickly supplied her with a visa, but the Czechs were different. Firstly my mother's application for a passport got 'lost'. She made another application. Nothing happened. She enquired why and was told by an official that someone had written a slanderous letter about her. My mother asked who, to be told solely that it was from 'an envious person'.

This angered me. I wrote a letter to Prague stating that I considered this an act of express distrust, which I did not intend to tolerate. My letter worked and a few weeks later my mother arrived at Heathrow Airport. But by now I had realized that the operation was not just a routine check. It went deeper than that.

Just before Christmas I heard through the Embassy grapevine that our Press Attaché, recently returned from Prague, Major Cerveny, had said to a friend that 'Joe will be recalled from London soon, believe you me.' Asked why, he had replied, 'Because in Prague they regard Joe as a security risk!'

Later I learned that a full-scale security operation had been launched against me that year under the direct control of no less a person than the new Minister of the Interior himself. Apparently I was suspected of having contacts with the British authorities, in particular with MI5. This was manifestly untrue. I was still racking my brains, trying to find a suitable means of defecting.

To the layman this might seem very simple. All the potential defector needed to do, one would imagine, was to walk out of the Embassy, approach the nearest policeman and say: 'Listen, my name is Josef Frolik. I am the Czech Labour Attaché in London. I want to defect.' Immediately the alert constable would spring into action. 'Phone calls would be made, Special Branch and MI5 would appear and our defector would be hurried away, smiling, happy and relieved, to some MI5 safe house in the suburbs.

But our layman underestimates the difficulties involved. There is the question of one's family, for instance. How would I get them together when I approached the constable? And if I could without rousing the suspicion of my comrades in Intelligence, could I rely on the constable responding promptly? Might I not meet a dummy who perhaps would think I was a drunk or who felt he needed orders from his superior officers before he could act? Even more frighteningly, might I chance upon one of those handful of London policemen who were in Czech pay? What then?

I had been long enough in the Intelligence business to know that my Service would, in this instance, stop at nothing—and I mean *nothing*—if it was thought I was going to defect. I knew far too much about the London operation now to be allowed to talk to MI5. They would not hesitate one moment. They would certainly use the final deterrent to seal my mouth.

Some of you reading this will probably be sceptical about that statement. That sort of stuff only goes on in spy thrillers! It never happens in real life! But it does—often. The history of Soviet and Eastern espionage is replete with examples of defecting agents being murdered in order to prevent them revealing what they knew. Way back in the 'twenties when James Bond was still in short pants, the Russian Ninth Section—Section for Terror and Diversion, to give it its official name—of the Second Directorate was already busy 'eliminating' important defectors. From the kidnapping of General Kutyepov from his flat in 1930, through the disappearance of Juliet Poyntz in New York and the killing of Ignace Reiss, to the murder of Trotsky in Mexico in May, 1940, the Russians repeatedly showed the length of their arm.

Immediately after the war they tried to kidnap the cipher clerk Gouzenko in their Canadian Embassy, after a terrible blunder on the part of the Canadian Mounted Police, through which the Russians learned that he wanted to defect. The same nearly occurred with Madam Petrov, after her husband had defected in

Australia, when Russian strong-arm men tried to force her on to a Soviet plane, an attempt which was foiled just in time by Australian photographers and TV cameramen. Then again there was the cold-blooded killing of the Ukrainian Leader (and agent of the Americans) Stephen Bandera in 1957 by the KGB agent Bogdan Stashinsky, who later confessed to the West Germans what he had done in Munich.

No, my defection had to be planned more carefully than that. And, besides, my wife was still hesitant. Her roots were in Czechoslovakia. Her English wasn't good and quite naturally she was tortured by the thought that if I defected, she would never see her family again. Constantly she urged me to have another go at trying to fit in. 'Let's go back,' she repeated time and time again, 'and see if we can live under the régime. If we can't, there'll always be another way out of Czechoslovakia'. And as a final example of typical female—and quite understandable—blackmail, she would point to our son and say sadly, 'And what will become of him if we have to run away?'

What indeed! But I knew in my heart that I could not continue much longer. I *had* to find a way out! Then unexpectedly that way out seemed to be offered to me on a platter.

On 30 December, 1965, I was invited to a party at the Embassy. The purpose of the party was twofold—the Embassy staff were going to celebrate the New Year and we were to honour the Commercial Department which had been awarded the Order of the Red Flag for its services to Anglo-Czech business. The drinking continued most of that gloomy winter afternoon, especially as the Ambassador honoured us with his noble presence. When it started to grow dark, I decided to go home. I had had enough to drink, my head was beginning to ache and I had promised my mother that I would take her to see the illuminations that evening.

I tried to excuse myself, but surprisingly enough Koska, who wasn't normally the life and soul of the party, wouldn't hear of it. 'No, no, you can't go now, Josef,' he said jovially. 'The night's still young.' So I stayed and had a few more. Now I was really beginning to feel my drinks and I tried once again to take my leave. 'Comrades,' I announced, rising to my feet somewhat unsteadily, 'I'm going home. My nut is about to fall off and I promised my mother that I'd show her the lights.'

There were cries of protest from the rest, but Koska no longer objected to my departure. 'You're quite right, Josef. You've had enough. But I'll tell you one thing, you're not driving yourself home in the state you're in. Come on.' And without waiting for me to object, he put his big boxer's paw on my arm. 'I'll run you home.'

Glad to have been allowed to go, I accepted the offer and staggered outside into the cold air towards his car. Koska, who appeared to be sober as far as I could judge, drove very carefully to the Bayswater Road and stopped at the corner of Queensway, not far from the fashionable Hungarian restaurant, the Mignon. I was just about to thank him for the lift and walk up the street to my flat, when he grabbed me and said, 'Come on, Josef, let's have a last one here.'

I tried to object, but he didn't give me a chance. I was hustled into the Mignon and within a matter of minutes found myself sitting in front of a bottle of heavy Hungarian red wine. My head was really swimming now and I said to Koska, 'God, I can't drink that stuff. My head's going to burst any moment.'

'We'll soon cure that, Josef,' he said heartily. 'Here, have a headache pill.' He thrust out a big hand containing a large pink pill which was unlike any headache tablet I had ever seen before. Fool that I was, I accepted it without hesitation. Time passed. How long I don't know. Suddenly the vague, swaying figure of Koska excused itself. 'Got to go to the lavatory, Josef.'

I nodded my understanding. Again time passed. But Koska did not return. Finishing the rest of my wine, I beckoned to the waiter and, thrusting some notes into his hand, staggered out of the place and headed up the Bayswater Road. Twenty metres, thirty metres, vaguely I could make out my front door. I fumbled for my keys. At that instant there was a tap on my shoulder and a voice said, 'I wonder if I could see your identification, sir?' My reaction was drunken but swift. I presume I acted in the way I did because I thought I was being attacked. Instinctively I swung round and launched a punch at the man's jaw, with all my two hundred pounds behind it. The policeman went down as if he had been pole-axed. The next moment a heavy truncheon landed on my head and everything went black.

SIX

The Interrogation

I woke up in a prison cell! My head felt terrible. Slowly, I tried to get up but I found I couldn't use my hands. Opening my eyes, I found out why. They were handcuffed. Then a young policeman came in and said curtly, 'Follow me.' My legs felt like jelly, but I managed to stagger into the next room, which was obviously the station's main office—clean, spartan and somehow threatening. Behind a desk sat another policeman, without a helmet. With a wave of his hand he indicated that I should sit down on one of the wooden chairs against the wall and opened his mouth to say something.

But I beat him to it. 'Where am I?' I asked.

'Paddington Police Station,' he said, adding that ominous 'Sir' which the British police use to even the most hardened criminals. Things didn't look too good, but I didn't have much time to consider the implications of the word, for at that moment a grey-haired, hard-faced man of about 55 entered the room and looked at me. Then he turned to the bare-headed policeman and held a whispered conversation with him for a few moments, before turning to me again.

'Mr Frolik?' he asked unnecessarily. I nodded.

'I'm a doctor,' the man said. 'How do you feel?'

'Not too bad,' I said. In reality, in spite of my wretched state, I was suddenly overcome with a sense of elation. I realized that this was the situation I had been waiting for all along. Here I was in the absolute safety of a British police station, with two policemen and a doctor in the offing, effectively cut off from my comrades, who undoubtedly would be well in their cups by now. *This was my chance to defect!*

Suddenly the 'doctor', who was definitely no doctor but a trained counter-intelligence man, brought his pale face close to

105

mine and hissed, 'Do you realize what you have done, Frolik? Not only did you knock out a British policeman, you also molested a woman. Even if she is only a prostitute, she is still entitled to protection against men like you!'

I looked up at him aghast. I remembered hitting the policeman well enough, but a woman? 'I don't remember any woman,' I stuttered. 'What am I supposed to have done?'

'Don't come that kind of tale with me,' the man snarled. 'You weren't that drunk. You know what you did, all right.' He licked the spittle off the corner of his mouth. 'Do you know what this will mean for you, Frolik?' he said menacingly.

'You've examined my wallet,' I exclaimed hurriedly, not a little frightened by the direction the conversation was taking. 'You must know that I am a diplomat and can claim diplomatic immunity.'

The civilian laughed mockingly. 'Did you hear that,' he called to the bareheaded policeman, 'He claims he's a diplomat! He's no more a diplomat than my foot is.' Turning to me again, he hissed, 'I'll tell you what you are, Frolik—*you're a spy!*'

A cold shudder ran down my spine. What was this all about? The man in front of me was playing some sort of game. But what? Was he an MI5 man, hurriedly summoned by the police when they discovered that I was a Czech diplomat, who was using my present miserable state to set me up? To set me up for what? Surely the treatment he was meting out to me would not exactly encourage me to co-operate? Or was there something more sinister behind the set-up, with the charge, out of the blue, that I had also roughed up some tart? The street had been completely deserted when I had tried to open the door to my flat.

But I knew that I couldn't back out now, whatever the man's motives were. I whispered, 'Please call the American Embassy for me. I have something to tell them. *Please!*'

Thereafter a strange silence descended on the room. The civilian continued to glare at me. But he asked no further questions, for which I was glad. I had burnt my boats. I had made my bid for freedom and must plan carefully the steps I would have to take from now on. First, naturally, I must insist that the Americans and/or the British spirit my family out of 34 Bayswater Road to some safe house. Then I must ensure that my former comrades did not know for at least a couple of days that I had defected, which wouldn't be too difficult over the New Year period. Those days would give me enough time to tell my future interrogators the details of the major Czech spies in the West so that they could be caught before they were warned. (I was determined to 'blow' the whole Czech network—as far as I knew it—in the West.) Finally I must obtain some guarantee from the Anglo-Americans that they would move us to America, as far away as possible from the long arm of Soviet retribution. That was essential, I knew, if I were going to survive the months of interrogation and de-briefing.

While all these thoughts were tumbling through my fevered brain, I kept glancing at my watch and then at the door of the station, waiting for the crew-cut head to appear, which would herald the arrival of the CIA. Time passed. Half an hour had gone by since they had promised to telephone the American Embassy. Still no American, and the Embassy was only a matter of minutes away in Grosvenor Square.

Another five minutes. Finally the door opened to admit a familiar but now terrifying figure. 'Hello, Josef,' he said in Czech, 'you've really got yourself into a juicy scandal this time, haven't you?' Jan Patek, the Ambassador's deputy smiled at me warmly.
The bastards had called the Czech Embassy!

Today, nearly ten years later, I still cannot account for the events of that strange 30 December. Later, when I recounted the episode to the men of MI5 and said a little mockingly, 'You missed a great chance then, gentlemen. I was really ready to defect then,' they looked at me as if I had gone mad. The grey-haired civilian had not been one of their men. They knew nothing at all about that strange interrogation by the 'doctor' in Paddington Police Station. Later, in the company of the MI5's top investigator, Jock Wilson of Special Branch, I went to Paddington Police Station. But our investigations drew a blank. There was no policeman there I could recognize as one of the two involved in my interrogation. Nor was there any station 'doctor' in any way resembling the one who had interrogated me. All that we could find was a brief entry in the station ledger which read: 'Indecent behaviour. Person claimed diplomatic immunity. Released in 35 minutes.' No more, no less!

Yet I had asked clearly enough to be put in touch with the US

Embassy, and in addition, a little note about our spy in the British Treasury had disappeared from my wallet. Why hadn't that call been placed and where had the incriminating paper gone? MI5 denied all knowledge of it.

If the arrest and the subsequent interrogation had not been the work of MI5, whose was it? Had Koska planned the whole thing. After all, he had also pulled the 'pink aspirin' trick on Benes, as I mentioned earlier. Why was he suddenly so solicitious about my well-being and why had he disappeared in the Mignon? Had he set me up for a counter-intelligence check? But if he had, how had he done it? British police stations are not normally readily available for hire by foreign intelligence services (though they may well be soon, the way things are going in the United Kingdom these days). And, in the final analysis, why hadn't Major Koska made anything of my attempt to call the American Embassy, which surely would have been related to him by the grey-haired civilian, if the latter had really been working for Koska? That, indeed, was the sixty-four-thousand-dollar question.[1]

As I say, I don't know the answers to any of the host of questions which that mysterious episode in Paddington occasions. But back in 1965 I was too frightened by what was to come to devote much time to them. What was going to happen now?

The answer was nothing—immediately.

On New Year's Eve, Husak welcomed me to the office with the friendly words: 'What a pig you are, Josef! Now you've got yourself into some real trouble.'

Koska, who was present, pacified him in his usual casual manner. 'Don't worry, Robert. I've got some friends in high places at the Home Office. There'll be no scandal.'

Wan, hollow-eyed and exceedingly worried, I nodded my thanks; I couldn't speak.

But Koska soon cleared the matter up. Together we drove to Paddington Police Station.

'Wait outside, Josef,' he ordered.

I needed no persuading. I'd seen enough of Paddington Police Station to last me a lifetime.

[1] There is only one other explanation I can think of: Koska was an agent for another intelligence service which wished to sound me out or blackmail me later into working for them. Which service that could be is beyond me.

Thirty very anxious minutes passed. Finally Koska bounced out of the station. He was smiling.

Climbing in beside me, he said: 'No problems, Josef. Everything's cleared up. There will be no protests from the British Foreign Office.'

I could not contain my heartfelt sigh of relief. A scandal had been avoided at least. Laughing like a couple of schoolboys just released from school, we drove off into the London traffic.

Two months later I was informed that my post in London had been terminated. I was to return home forthwith.

The Prague Spring (1966–1969)

'He, the trained spy, had walked into the trap
For a bogus guide, seduced with the old tricks.'
W. H. Auden

ONE

A School for Spies

When I returned to Prague in March, 1966, I knew for sure that I was under surveillance. My personal effects, arriving from London under customs seals, had been broken into en route and examined. There was no doubt about that. But that was only the start. On the pretext of getting my flat ready for me, my case officer had borrowed the keys from my relatives and given them to the technical department, who immediately went to work to bug the place. They did it so clumsily that one of them bumped into a neighbour of mine late at night in the attic above my flat. When challenged, the technician said that he was a telephone repair man who had entered the attic by the skylight from a neighbouring building. His excuse was that he hadn't wanted to climb down and up five flights of stairs to reach the attic. He had overlooked the fact that at that time of night both buildings were locked to everyone, except naturally to State Security people.

Finally some anonymous wellwisher informed me by telephone that I had had visitors in my apartment prior to my return. I thanked my informant and hung up, wondering anxiously what I had let myself in for by returning to my native country.

I found out the next day when I reported for duty. Taborsky started to attack me at once. 'You didn't work at all at your official target in London, Frolik!' he said accusingly. 'Half the time you were fussing around with trade union leaders instead of getting on with the job assigned to you.'

I have always been a great believer in the theory that attack is the best form of defence. So I immediately let loose at him. 'Now you listen to me,' I replied angrily. 'You know as well as I do what is happening over there in London. Half of your men are crooks lining their own nests. Look at Koska, for instance, padding expenses all the time, inventing and paying agents who don't exist. And you are covering up for those people!'

That did it. Avoiding my gaze, he said in a calmer voice, 'Let's forget it, Frolik. I asked you here to tell you that your NATO assignment has been abolished.'

'I see,' I replied in a non-committal tone. 'And what's my next assignment?'

He shrugged. 'Well, one thing is certain—there is no post free for you here in the British department.' It didn't take a mind-reader to realize that Taborsky was trying to get rid of me in case I was later arrested as a suspect; he didn't want to be involved. 'However, there is a job going in the new department we've just set up.'

'What's that?'

'To work against the CIA.'

But the job turned out to be a strictly administrative one, which I didn't like a bit. Knowing now that I had nothing to lose, I went to see my old boss Jodas who had just taken charge of Directorate B of the Main Directorate of Intelligence. 'Listen,' I told him, 'I'm being given the run-around here, and I think I know why.' I took the bull by the horns. 'Because they think—at least, that's what I surmise—that I'm working for the British.'

Jodas laughed out loud. 'Go on!' he gasped. 'Not *you*, Josef!'

'Oh, yes they do,' I maintained firmly, realizing that I had found an ally.

'Impossible,' Colonel Jodas said. 'But don't worry, Josef. I'll find you a job in my department.'

Thus it was that I was transferred to Jodas' Department of Intelligence Games and first got to know about the spy school and its pupils.

But still the surveillance went on. Just about then I took my wife off on a long weekend. When we returned, our bedroom stank of French cologne. Someone had overturned and broken a bottle of scent during a search. We couldn't sleep in the bedroom for days afterwards.

A little while later I discovered a fresh set of 'bugs' in the wall of my living-room. Then one evening, when we were all watching TV, I decided to give my brother-in-law, who was present, a drink of Scotch, a great treat in Czechoslovakia. The night before I had opened a new bottle. Now, when I fetched it, there was only a drop at the bottom. Obviously, during a search, one of the team had been unable to withstand the temptation. As I remarked to my wife ruefully, 'I hope it kept the poor soul warm!'

Then, for no apparent reason, the surveillance stopped. Had it something to do with the changing political climate in Czechoslovakia which was soon to bring about Novotny's downfall? I didn't know then, just as I don't know now. One thing I do know, however—two months later the surveillance started again. But this time it was being carried out by another service and another nation—*the Russians*![1]

But I had other things to worry about besides the surveillance team. After all, in a communist country most people are under surveillance at one time or another; such a thing is not as nerve-racking as it would be in a Western country. Luckily I had a devil of a lot of work in my new assignment, trying to find agents for a completely new sphere of operations for Czech Intelligence, namely Africa. It was a sign of the growing importance of the Middle East and the newly independent African countries. Just like our American rivals, the CIA, we were scrambling desperately to infiltrate key agents into important posts in the new countries, which had until recently been the colonies of the European powers. But, unlike the Americans, we had several thousand potential recruits right under our noses, for the Czech Government, in all its selfless generosity, had established the 'Seventeenth of November University' in Prague on the model of the Moscow-based Patrice Lumumba University.

Here were 4,500 students, predominantly coloured, from all over Africa and the Middle East, who had come to Czechoslovakia to study the normal subjects one does at university, as well as to be indoctrinated, whether they liked it or not, in communist theory and practice. Before being allowed to attend this 'university', the would-be student had to attend a one-year preparatory course in the Czech language. Here he would be checked as to his fitness for recruitment to the Intelligence Service. If he were found suitable, he would continue his studies at the University, but at the same time he would be schooled for his

[1] Already concerned with the way things were going in Czechoslovakia, they were sounding out certain key people, who might help or harm them in the critical days ahead. Naturally we of Intelligence came into this category.

future role as a spy, ready for infiltration into his own country's infrastructure.

The Seventeenth of November University proved a tremendous source of material for us and I don't think it would be going too far to say that half the students had contacts with Czech Intelligence at one time or other. But we had our headaches with these dusky visitors to Central Europe.

Take, for instance, Dakar who came from Pemba Island, part of the new United Republic of Tanzania, where he was a friend of many highly placed officials and Ministers. He was recruited by our people shortly after his arrival in Prague, where he was studying medicine. Unfortunately he failed his first year and was expelled, not because he was stupid but because he liked a good time—with the aid of the money paid to him by us—which included fathering a little Dakar by a blonde Czech shopgirl. Our service finally sent him to Dar-es-Salaam, where it was his task to locate and photograph CIA safe houses in the city. He completed the task exceedingly well, even staying at the house of a Minister and bringing back with him important political information as well as photos of the houses in which the CIA used to meet their agents.

Unfortunately success went to his head, and at the time when I took him over he was no longer interested in medicine; he liked the life and money of a spy too much. I sent him on a couple of missions to Poland and to Cairo, but he wasn't much good. So I decided to drop him as untrustworthy and idle. Thus it was that he came into contact with a mysterious Irishman living in Prague, a native of Eire named Brian Devlin.

Devlin seemed to have plenty of money, which he spent liberally in the Prague nightspots. Soon he started spending it on Dakar too. One night, after this disparate twosome had known each other for some while, Devlin got Dakar very drunk and then asked if the latter would sell him his passport. At first the African refused. But more drinks followed and Devlin explained to him that all he would have to do if he sold the passport would be to go to his Embassy and say that he had lost it; in due course they would give him another one. So Dakar gave in and sold his passport to Devlin. The next morning, however, he had a change of heart. He was scared he might have trouble with Czech Intelligence if they found out what he had done. So he took a taxi to Devlin's flat and demanded his passport back. In the end the Irishman returned it to him, saying that it had only been a trick to test him out. When Dakar told me what had happened—somewhat shamefacedly—I didn't think it was a joke. I wrote to State Security and asked them to investigate the matter.

But the matter was sorted out sooner than I expected. A couple of days later Devlin and Dakar were in an expensive restaurant having supper, next to a table where some Hungarians were having a farewell celebration. Drink flowed freely at both tables and all of them soon got pretty drunk. Dakar then decided to dance with a pretty blonde Czech who, shortly before, had refused to dance with one of the Hungarians. The man did not take her acceptance of Dakar's request lightly. As the coloured man whirled by with the girl, he tried to kick his feet from under him. But he was too drunk to make contact. So he waited until Dakar returned to his table and then gave him such a wallop that he slid across the dance floor and blacked out for a moment. When he recovered, Dakar picked up an empty bottle from his own table and smashed it across the Hungarian's head. Now it was the Hungarian's turn to black out. The fun had started! Like any good Irishman Devlin could not resist a fight. He flung himself into the scrap and in an instant the restaurant was in chaos with waiters shouting, women screaming and bodies flying everywhere. Ten minutes later the police arrived and arrested the whole bunch.

An ordinary tavern brawl, one might conclude. But back in the police cells, the ramifications started to emerge. In broken Czech Devlin asked if he might call someone on the General Staff of the People's Army, while one of the Hungarians insisted on calling his Embassy. In despair, the Captain in charge called me and put me in the picture, concluding, 'It's like a brothel down here. One of them claims he's your agent, another turns out to be an agent of the General Staff and the Hungarians are something important in their service. I'm going to fine each of them five hundred crowns and kick the bastards out!'

'Well don't think I'm coming down there to pay Dakar's fine,' I said, a little annoyed at being woken at that time of the morning. 'Let the Hungarian Embassy do it—they've got plenty of money.'

'But they won't,' the Captain protested.

'Then charge it to the army.'

The harassed Captain agreed to do so, as a Colonel of the

General Staff was coming to bail Devlin out. Later I discovered that not only did he pay Devlin's fine, but that of everyone else concerned; obviously Devlin was an important man.

Accordingly I went over to see the Colonel in question and told him about Devlin's approach to my man Dakar. 'My dumb Irishman didn't even realize that Dakar was an Intelligence agent,' the Colonel exclaimed. 'Otherwise the fool wouldn't have made the approach.'

Thus, unwittingly, my drunken playboy-agent had led me to another agent being run as an 'illegal', obviously for later employment in Ireland, by Czech Military Intelligence.[1] Today, I often wonder what part the mysterious Mr Devlin is playing in IRA activities in Ulster, at the command of his spymaster in far-off Prague?

Another agent, recruited from the spy school, whom I ran at that time was George. Like Dakar he was black, coming from Kenya, and a member of the Kikuyu Tribe. He was recruited early and like Dakar grew very friendly with a Czech girl by whom he had two beautiful children. Unlike my other agent, however, he married the girl. The girl's father, a pre-war communist, hit the ceiling when he heard of the marriage. Angrily he maintained that his 'poor' girl had been 'prostituted by the black bastard'. In fact, his 'poor girl' had a respectable record as a street walker in the Prague police files. But the old man's continual harassment finally made George only too glad to go on a mission for us, though he didn't need to because he had independent means. So I sent the former Mau-Mau terrorist—he'd joined the movement as a boy—off to Dar-es-Salaam where he was to infiltrate the CIA. He did so without hesitation, actually visiting the CIA agent so that he could check him and his house out under the pretext of wanting to buy his car. He also checked the CIA agent's contacts, meeting-places with other agents, etc. In short, he carried out a perfectly successful intelligence mission. Indeed his case officer out there, Captain Milan Lieskovsky, could not praise him enough.

[1] Illegals, in contrast to 'Legals' (who operate from an embassy cover, as I did in London), have no connection with the officials of their country abroad. So, while I knew the legal network in the UK, I had no idea of the extent of the 'illegal' activity.

But, in spite of this, George, like Dakar and all the other black products of the Seventeenth of November University, were problem children for me, continually getting themselves into trouble over money and women, especially the Arabs, who proved time and again to be greedy, cowardly and treacherous—and worse. In 1967 they started to carry on their private feuds in the streets of Prague, as we shall see in the next chapter.

TWO

The Jordan Murder

On a bright sunny day in August, 1967, Prague received an important visitor from the United States, a square-jawed, bespectacled American named Charles Jordan, who was the Director-General of the Zionist Joint Distribution Committee for Jewish Relief. But official Prague decided that it did not want to acknowledge his presence; the Six Day War between Israel and Egypt had just ended in defeat for the latter and a wave of anti-semitism was sweeping from Moscow westwards through the Warsaw Pact countries.

But if Prague did not wish to acknowledge the prominent Zionist's presence, there were others who had been aware of it even before he arrived—Palestinian guerrillas who had been trailing him through Rumania, where he had been before he reached Czechoslovakia on 14 August. Now they 'passed him over' to their colleagues in Prague—the same young men we were training at the Seventeenth of November University. Within the Egyptian Embassy, then the headquarters of the Palestinians in Prague, hasty plans began to be made.

During the evening of 16 August Charles Jordan found he had run out of cigarettes. Turning to his wife he said casually, 'I'll just pop out, honey, and buy some cigarettes.' Leaving the Esplanade Hotel, he set off down George Washington Street—and vanished. When he didn't turn up, his wife enquired at the Esplanade's desk. From there the matter went to the American Embassy. The Americans immediately called in Czech State Security, but they knew nothing. A search was instituted. Then on 20 August, Major Habetin's River Division of Public Security fished a dead body out of the River Vltava. It was identified within the hour as that of Charles Jordan.

The Czech Government ordered an immediate post-mortem.

120

Its findings were that Mr Jordan had died of drowning. No marks of violence or evidence of drugs were found. As the official statement had it, it was assumed that Jordan had committed suicide by throwing himself into the Vltava.

There was an immediate outcry in the West, especially in America. Why, people asked, would he travel a thousand miles to throw himself into an obscure river. Jordan had been murdered on the orders of the Czech Government.

The post-mortem was repeated by an independent pathologist, a Swiss doctor named Ernst Hardmeier. It was a very unfortunate mission for him, for when he found traces of a drug in the dead man's pancreas, he unwittingly signed his own death warrant.

A little while later he went off on a holiday into the mountains in his native country, where he simply lay down in the snow near his car and froze to death. Another case of suicide, the Czechs said. I doubt it. For Dr Hardmeier had discovered something which the Czech Government was trying hard to cover up, namely that the prominent Zionist had not committed suicide—he had been murdered!

When Jordan left his hotel that evening he had hardly gone a dozen yards down George Washington Street when a car pulled to a halt beside him. Four swarthy men jumped out, bundled him into the car and drove off at high speed—in full view of three car-loads of Czech security men who had been watching Jordan because it was thought in Intelligence that he was an Israeli spy! But if they didn't interfere with this first operation of the Palestinian guerrillas behind the Iron Curtain, they did radio their HQ that Jordan had been abducted in a car which belonged to the Egyptian Embassy. The head of the 4th Directorate of the State Security, Colonel Antonin Kavan, who had once tried to arrest Barak, ordered them to take up the chase and observe what was going on. But the Egyptian diplomat's car didn't go far. It pulled up outside the Egyptian Embassy and the Czechs watched as the kidnappers dragged their captive inside. Thereupon the security men took up their positions at every possible exit from the Embassy so that no one could leave unobserved. An infra-red camera, used for photographing at night, was hastily brought up and the watchers settled back to wait.

Their vigil ended in the early hours of the following morning, by which time the whole of the Czech Service and the Govern-

E

ment, including Novotny, had been informed. At about three the Embassy back door was opened to reveal the kidnappers carrying out Jordan's body. Immediately the infra-red camera was put into operation and the whole business was photographed without the kidnappers knowing a thing. They drove down to the Vltava about half a mile away and tossed in the corpse. Wiping their hands, as if satisfied with their work, they got back into their car and returned to the Embassy.

The next morning the Minister of the Interior had the watchers' full report, the incriminating photos, and the identities of the three Palestinians who had carried out the kidnapping on his desk. But he was not very happy with them. They placed him in a terrible fix. The reports made it quite clear that Jordan had been murdered by the Palestinians at the Embassy, where they had used scopalomine injections to make him talk. But dare he incriminate an ally by announcing the fact to the world? More, if he did so, he would indirectly incriminate his own service; for had not eleven officers, equipped with automatics and radio equipment, stood tamely by and watched Jordan being abducted? What would the world have to say about that?

In the end Vladimir Koucky, then secretary of the Czech Communist Party's Central Committee, summoned the Egyptian Ambassador to see him. He told the Ambassador that Czechoslovakia would neither demand the murderers from the Egyptians nor inform the Americans what had really happened. 'Czechoslovakia,' he said 'is not interested in spoiling her relations with the Arab states nor in engendering sympathy for the Jews,' with whom the Czech Government itself had problems. All that Koucky asked was that the murderers should leave the country as quickly and as quietly as possible. To this the much relieved Ambassador agreed. Three days later the three Palestinian 'students' left for the German Democratic Republic to continue their 'studies'.

Thus the murder was hushed up at the highest level. Novotny had naturally had to give his personal approval to the solution of the problem—and Prague brazened it out to the bitter end, although the Swiss doctor's testimony was proof enough of what had really happened.

THREE

The Day of the Jackal

Another operation which showed that murderers were in charge of the Czech state in the late 'sixties was the plan to murder President de Gaulle.

Back in the early 'sixties, Eastern political leaders had realized that the French President, so eager to restore to France her traditional *Gloire*, could be used for the achievement of their major policy aim in the West, namely to split Europe from the United States and thus break up NATO, which stood between them and domination of Western Europe.

De Gaulle's treatment during his wartime exile had made him no friend of either England or the United States. 'Joan of Arc', as Roosevelt called him behind his back, soon showed that he was prepared to pay back real and imagined insults once he attained power in 1958. He subverted Adenauer from his pro-American stand by offering him the friendship of France; he broke away from NATO; and by his provocative speech to the French Canadians he made it quite clear what he felt about his former American allies who had saved France in 1944.

Naturally our Intelligence was aware of this. We were also aware that there were a good number of individuals and organizations which would have been only too glad to get rid of the General. In particular, the semi-fascist OAS, defeated in the bloody, bitter war in Algeria, was thirsting for the blood of the man whom they felt had betrayed them.

Several times de Gaulle narrowly escaped cunningly worked-out murder plans by right-wing individuals and organizations,[1] but whereas the OAS had to work without any internal help in the formation of their assassination operations, the Soviets had someone at the very top of French counter-intelligence, who

[1] In all, I believe, there were thirty-one attempts on his life in those years.

could give them all the 'inside' information they needed. That someone is known as 'Topaz' in Leon Uris's book of the same name. In actual fact he was (and still is) known by his KGB masters as 'Saphyr'; *he is still working in French counter-intelligence to this very day*, in spite of the fact that the French authorities were informed of his real allegiance by the Anglo-Americans as soon as the French diplomat, Philippe de Vosjoli, defected to the USA. But then the French never believe anything from 'perfidious Albion' and, now, perfidious America.

In one of the last attempts on de Gaulle's life, the would-be assassin was caught and was soon singing like a bird—the French are not exactly timid in the methods of interrogation which they use. During questioning he mentioned that he was an agent of the CIA, though he pointed out specifically that he had not carried out the assassination attempt on the orders of the CIA, but at the command of his own organization, the OAS. Nevertheless, Saphyr jumped on the connection with the CIA and in his report to the President (the KGB agent was such a high-level official that he could prepare reports directly for de Gaulle!) he emphasized the CIA participation in the plot to such an extent that the President was convinced that the Americans were out to get him.

The seeds had been sown for the operation which Czech Intelligence now planned.

During the Six Day War, de Gaulle, who was usually regarded as pro-Arab, took a markedly neutral attitude: something which irritated the Palestinians. It also gave Czech Intelligence the idea that they could use de Gaulle to discredit the United States and stir up more trouble in the Middle East.

Under the leadership of Colonel Josef Jindrich, alias Janous, chief of the Afro-Asian Department of our Intelligence Service, with whom I had quite a lot to do through my work with African agents, it was decided to assassinate the French President when he went on a visit to Beirut, a trip which had been planned for some time.

Our people assumed, correctly, that he would not miss the opportunity to pay his respects to the French dead of two wars buried in the French Cemetery just outside Beirut. In particular he would undoubtedly want to place a wreath on the war memorial there. Accordingly Jindrich ordered that some means

124

should be found of setting an explosive charge under the memorial, which would go off at the exact moment that de Gaulle bent to place his wreath on the stone. In Beirut our 'resident', Major Jansky, began to work out the details and find a suitable Palestinian commando to carry out the plan, so that Czech Intelligence did not need to be physically involved in case it came unstuck.

The problem was solved quickly enough. Jansky went to work on his contacts within the Beirut Police, in particular, its chief, who was a Soviet agent. These men were to find the 'proof' that the murder had been planned by the CIA. In addition, they would have to manufacture evidence that the CIA had been working hand-in-glove with the Israeli Intelligence Service, Mossad. Thus when the assassination had been carried out, both America and Israel would be implicated in the murder. The result would be a wave of anti-American and anti-Israeli feeling, not only through France but probably throughout Western Europe as well. Israel's days as an independent nation would then undoubtedly be numbered. Thus Jindrich's reasoning, by which he persuaded the President of Czechoslovakia to sanction the operation.

The wheels began to turn until everything was ready. All Jindrich needed now was the victim! But then fate took a hand in the game. Just before President de Gaulle was due to journey to Lebanon, events in France occasioned him to call a referendum. To his chagrin—and that of the planners in Prague—he lost the referendum. In a fit of pique he resigned his high office and was thus unable to pay his long-planned visit to Lebanon.

As a result, the old soldier died in bed of natural causes and Israel survived to fight another day.

FOUR

Bakalar

I, for one, was glad the operation failed, not only because I respected the old man, but also because it would undoubtedly have shaken the whole of the Middle East and perhaps have 'blown' the most senior agent I had ever 'run'.

That agent was Abdul Al Barri, known by his cover-name of Bakalar, a Syrian, who was Chief of the Department of the Government Praesidium in Damascus. Bakalar had first come to my notice when he warned one of our men in Damascus that some of the Arab students attending the Seventeenth of November University in Prague were, in fact, in the pay of Western Intelligence agencies. We worked on the tip and at the same time investigated the man who had sent us the information. We discovered three things—that Bakalar had attended the University himself and had married a Czech nurse; that in his official position he was filling the government administration with men loyal to his uncle, General Hafez Assad, then Minister of National Defence;[1] and that his real aim in life was to prepare for a take-over of power by his uncle. In other words Bakalar was a man worthy of cultivation. I determined to do that cultivating when the time was ripe.

The time came in October, 1967, when General Assad paid a state visit to Czechoslovakia. With him he brought Bakalar. So on the night of the official reception given by our Minister of Defence, General Lomsky, I gate-crashed the party. I was soon turfed out—at first I got a royal reception because our people thought I was part of the Syrian party—but not before I had had time to make an initial contact with Bakalar.

A few days later I met him at the home of his parents-in-law and liked him straight away. He was an honourable, educated

[1] Today President of the Syrian Republic.

man, totally unlike the other Arabs I had dealt with so far. He had a straightforward character and was completely without that Arab slyness which I had come to dislike intensely.

Our discussion was brief and pertinent. All that both of us were concerned with was to agree on certain guarantees. For a start he wanted protection for any of his countrymen in Czechoslovakia who might be discovered working for the West. We, for our part, wanted an assurance that we would be the sole recipients of his information. From that day onwards he worked completely gratis, so unlike my other Arab agents who were always asking for more and more money. All I ever gave Bakalar was a few weapons, which he treasured, as, for example, the newest Czech sub-machine-gun at that time, the *Skorpion*.

For over a year Bakalar kept me supplied with top-level information about affairs in Syria, which were of the utmost importance in the communist camp because of the extremely tense situation in the Middle East. He filled us in on the details of the Syrian–Egyptian relationships; who supported the fascist Ba'ath Party run by Aflak; who were the supporters of the Syrian communist leader Khaled Bakdash; who was trying, without success, to convince the Soviets that they should lend their major support to Syria and not to Egypt. The reports also covered the country's internal affairs and the work of foreign intelligence services in Syria. For example, he transmitted copies of the interrogation record of the most famous Israeli agent in the country, Eli Cohen, who was later executed for espionage in Damascus. And he informed us of the extensive Soviet KGB network in Syria, which included not only the President, Nur-ad-Din Atassi, but also the Chief-of-Security, Colonel Jundi.

Naturally, as this information was of such high quality, I sent it up until it reached some of the top officials in the country. But to my surprise, it did not receive their approval—not one bit of it! Instead the details of the KGB network and the base behaviour of the Soviet Ambassador to Syria aroused their wrath: something which puzzled me a little.

Indeed six months after Bakalar had begun to co-operate with us I was summoned by the Deputy Chief of Czech Intelligence, Colonel Jindrich, and told angrily, 'We are constantly discovering, Florian (my cover name), that you are trying to disrupt the friendly relations which exist between the Soviet Union and Syria.

You are always trying to make mountains out of molehills with this Bakalar fellow of yours!'

'What do you mean, Comrade Colonel?' I asked, astonished by the vehemence of his attack.

'You know exactly what I mean, Florian! You exaggerate what's going on over there and you use Bakalar as a mouthpiece for your own anti-Soviet hate.'

I grew angry in my turn. What the devil was the Colonel up to, trying to defend the Soviet Union like this? After all, he was a Czech. 'Colonel,' I said, trying to control my rage, 'are you speaking as a representative of Czech Intelligence or as the mouthpiece of Soviet propaganda?'

Jindrich flushed. 'You just watch it, Florian!' he roared. 'I'll soon clip your wings if you don't.'

'As far as I know, Colonel,' I bellowed back, 'you are still the head of the Afro-Asian Department and not my immediate boss. I am an intelligence officer and I believe the job of an intelligence officer is to find out the truth, however painful it might be.' I took a deep breath, and said, 'If you don't like the information Bakalar is supplying us, then from now onwards you can rely on the information you get from Chlad.[1] From today you'll get no more from Bakalar—that I can assure you, *Comrade* Colonel!'

And with that I turned and left, leaving Jindrich fuming at his desk. But if I had had the satisfaction of scoring the last point against Jindrich, I was still completely puzzled why he should take up the defence of Soviet Intelligence in Syria in such an aggressive and menacing manner. What had it got to do with him?

My bewilderment was increased a few weeks later when I received a hurried and alarmed report from Bakalar that an attempt had been made on his life. One evening he had had an appointment with his Czech handling officer in Damascus, a Major August. Returning home to the suburbs in the twilight, he was met by three men in an open jeep who fired wild bursts of machine-gun fire at his car. He braked to a halt and flung himself down as if he had been shot. The would-be murderers did not wait to find out. With a squeal of tyres, they were off—only to run slap into a patrol of Syrian security men. The latter opened

[1] Another of our Syrian agents, who was a member of the local communist party and also a KGB agent, as I was to find out later.

128

up instinctively and within seconds two of the killers were dead and the third, his white shirt stained with his comrades' blood, had his hands in the air, begging for mercy.

The Syrians immediately went to work on the third man, using what we delicately called 'unselective means', and the bird started to sing. Within the hour he had admitted that the assassination plot had been planned by none other than the Chief-of-Security, Colonel Jundi himself! Not only had Jundi wanted to assassinate Bakalar, he had also aimed at killing Assad, who was going to visit his nephew's house that same evening. Immediately the news was relayed to Bakalar who, taking the bull by the horns, phoned Colonel Jundi and told him what he knew.

Jundi broke down completely. He knew what his fate would be if he fell into the hands of Assad. Pleading for mercy, he stated that the operation had not really been planned by himself, but by his masters in the KGB.[1]

When I received the report, I was shocked. Why, I asked myself in bewilderment, would the Russians attempt to kill a man whose vital information was also being relayed to them? What were the Soviets up to? I was soon to find out.

As 1967 gave way to 1968, Soviet attempts to drive a wedge between Bakalar and myself escalated. At that time Syria was interested in getting a large delivery of Czech anti-aircraft guns, which had proved effective in the air defence of Damascus against Israeli jets, and were prepared to pay hard dollars for them. The deal had already gone through when suddenly the Soviets stepped in and said 'nyet'; the delivery of the guns would weaken the Warsaw Pact's defensive capability. Assad immediately sent Bakalar to Prague to obtain my help in the matter. Naturally, Bakalar said, the continuation of our relationship depended upon the delivery. I took up the matter with the State Secretary of the Ministry of Defence, Lt-General Dvorak. He said he'd look into it, but the next day he informed me that the Soviet representative for the Warsaw Pact at the Russian Embassy in Prague had again vetoed the shipment. But the General's look showed me just how threadbare he thought the Soviet excuse.

Later, at a dinner I had arranged in Bakalar's honour in my

[1] When Bakalar told Colonel Jundi that he would be shown no mercy, the latter said he would never be taken alive. Putting down the telephone, he shot himself there and then.

apartment, I told him the bad news, explaining that I, personally, could see no reason why the Soviets wanted to stop the shipment. He was very far from pleased.

A few days later I saw him for the last time. Now he really laid it on the line. He told me that the Russians intended to break off the contacts we had with the Syrians. They had turned down the Syrian request for the establishment of a Syrian Intelligence training school on Czech soil. Then, a week or two later, a whole planeload of East German Intelligence agents had suddenly turned up out of the blue in Damascus. Their appearance had caused a minor scandal; no one had asked for them and no one expected them. Finally, after a few days, they had all returned to Berlin, save one, who went to work on Bakalar. While out shooting one day, he tried to bribe Bakalar with a new Peugeot 404, a hand-tooled hunting rifle and regular monthly payments. Then he told Bakalar that the Soviets were interested in having the East Germans take over the role of the Czechs in Syria.

At that last meeting, Bakalar looked at me with a mixture of anger and sadness. 'Florian,' he said, 'I understand your position *vis-à-vis* the Soviets very well. You are the underdogs just as the Soviets think we are in Syria.'

I nodded glumly. That very day, I had been refused an official vehicle to drive Bakalar to the airport, just to remind me who was in charge.

'But don't think we Syrians are going to give in to Russian pressure, just as some of your own leaders do continually . . .'

I held up my hand in protest. 'Our people will soon get rid of those corrupt leaders,' I said quickly.

He shrugged in his Arab way. 'Perhaps, but I will tell you one thing, Florian. We Syrians are going to find another way out of our difficulties, believe you me. My advice to you Czechs is to do the same before it is too late and big brother swallows you up!'

How prophetic those words were! But I didn't realize it then. All I was concerned with was the loss of my key agent. Two weeks after Bakalar's abortive trip to Prague, a Syrian military mission under the command of the Syrian Chief-of-Staff, Major-General Tlas, flew to Peking to start negotiations with Red China.

Perhaps I may be allowed a brief digression here. Although it is often thought that Russia is anti-Israeli and pro-Arab, this is

Accordingly Alexandr met the 'British journalist', who spoke with a strong American accent. The 'Britisher' did not beat about the bush. He asked straightaway for information about the first Czech nuclear electric power plant at Jaselske Bohunice, which, because its construction was proceeding so slowly, was thought in the West to be of enormous size. In fact the plant, which was started in 1956, was finally completed in 1974. Thanks to the 'invaluable aid' of the Russians in its construction and the necessity of buying back our own uranium from our 'socialist brothers' in the East, construction advanced at a snail's pace. Indeed, as one of my associates said, 'It's almost as if an Amazon tribe were constructing a Boeing 747—without tools.'

But the 'Britisher', who turned out to be a Mr E. New of the US Consulate in Bombay, didn't know this—so he was interested. Alexandr passed on what he knew and was duly rewarded. Naturally he passed on the information to his superior and it was decided to initiate an intelligence game with Mr Choura. Thus he came into our lives.

I first met Mr Choura in 1966 when he came to Prague to protest that his business partners there had not received permission from the Czech government to transfer £70,000 they owed him in sterling to his account in Barclays Bank, London; apparently they feared there might be a devaluation of the Indian rupee. I was ordered to contact him at the Hotel International, under the pretence of being a member of the Ministry of Foreign Affairs, to discuss the matter and to have a look at him.

The meeting went off well. I promised to try to help him with his currency problems and we arranged to meet again. Apparently taking a liking to me, he said he felt he could give me some interesting information. 'Do you mean intelligence information?' I asked, looking shocked. He grinned at me, all white teeth and dark rolling eyes. Yes, he did. I said I appreciated the offer and would inform my chief accordingly.

Thereupon we arranged a third meeting, which took place the next day. Slowly Mr Choura started to warm to his subject. He had plenty of 'good friends' in US Embassies everywhere. Of course they weren't spies. But he assumed they were always looking for information that would help the United States. Naturally he was friendly with them, but he would never aid them. After all he was a communist and most of his profits flowed into

133

the coffers of the Indian Communist Party. Hadn't he played a big part in financing the election campaign of a well-known Indian politician, Mr Krishna Menon? On and on the babble flowed.

In the end, I got bored. 'Mr Choura,' I interrupted, 'May I introduce myself? I am a Czech Intelligence officer. My name is Florian.'

He stopped immediately. His mouth flopped open and he stared at me as if I had just announced I'd arrived from Mars.

I then told him that we had a sizable file on him, which did not exactly show him up in a good light, to say the least of it. That really sobered him up and he began telling the truth. He was, as we had suspected, a CIA agent who worked under the cover of being a loyal member of the Indian Communist Party and a friend and informant of Czech Intelligence.

When I parted with Mr Choura he was indeed an official member of Czech Intelligence, under the cover name of Igl. (He had wanted the name 'Roy', but I felt that was too grand for him!) We planned to use him to penetrate enemy headquarters by recruiting his CIA case officer. That would really be a feather in the cap of Czech Intelligence if we could pull it off.

First of all we let him visit his contacts in Western Europe and call on his CIA European case officer in Vienna. Thereafter, I met him in Karlovy Vary (Carlsbad), where he had gone to take the waters; he suffered from liver trouble, and hoped the famous Czech springs would cure him. He had other problems, which could not be cured so easily. During one session at the spa, he confessed to me that he had never slept with a woman in his life; he was a homosexual. Could we arrange for some sort of 'cure' for that 'complaint' as well?

I promised that we would 'look into it', and urged him to start writing his memoirs, which were vital to us if we were to carry out our intended ploy correctly.

And so, against this unusual background, where kings and queens had once come to redress the balance of their over-indulgence, my fat Indian fairy began to 'sing'. And he knew a lot. He told me all about the CIA's co-operation with the Indian Police; how the two groups had tried to arrange the defection of a couple of KGB officers; how the CIA had effectively ensured the division of the Indian Communist Party into splinter groups—

pro-Soviet, pro-Chinese, nationalist, Trotskyite, etc. My chief was delighted with the memoirs, and before Choura went on his way, he was informed that his money would be allowed to go to Barclays in London.

I saw him again a few months later when he reported that he had been interrogated by the CIA in a safe house in the western half of Berlin. This worried me. Had he spilled the details of his association with Czech Intelligence? I decided to drive to East Berlin to check. It was a nightmare journey, with the roads metre-high with new snow. When I finally arrived, I asked our Resident whether it would be possible to give the Indian a lie-detector test in a safe house, secure against the pryings of the CIA, who seemed to be everywhere.

Eventually I was taken to a decrepit house not far from the Wall, where two of our men listened to and recorded West German Police and other Intelligence Services' radio traffic all day long. Here we could carry out the test in safety. But Choura did not turn up. Nor did he appear at a subsequent rendezvous arranged by myself in Czechoslovakia. Another rendezvous was fixed up in Bulgaria. Still no Choura. I began to wonder what kind of game he was playing. Had he gone back to his former masters and thus stymied our whole scheme? Or had my rash, off-the-cuff offer to arrange some sort of treatment for his homosexuality frightened him off? I knew he was still seeing his boyfriend in Denmark in spite of his apparent desire to be 'cured'.

Suddenly other events occurred which drove all thoughts of the elusive Mr Choura from my mind—a complete change of Government in Czechoslovakia. The 'Prague Spring' had arrived.

The ultimate confrontation between the Czechoslovak people and the morally discredited, economically bankrupt and politically hated Novotny régime began at about the time of the Arab-Israeli conflict in June, 1967, when the Czech writers expressed their dissatisfaction at the postponement of their Annual Congress. A resolution was approved which deplored, among other things, the Government's attitude to the Jews and proclaimed sympathy with their cause.

The publication of the Congress resolution was banned, even in the writers' own paper, *Literary News*, so a group of intellectuals, organized by a certain Dr Ivan Pfaff, issued a secret document which embodied the main findings of the Congress and the true aspirations of the writers' and artists' community. This was then smuggled abroad and published on the front page of *The Sunday Times* on 3 September, and in the *New York Times* on the following day, and then began to make the rounds of the world's press.

Dr Pfaff, discovered as the main organizer, was taken into custody but refused to name his accomplices. A clever Government adviser made him sign a declaration to the effect that he was the only person responsible, and thus the régime concealed the fact that the Manifesto represented the feelings of a great number of writers and cultural workers.[1]

After this, the Czech students took to the streets, ostensibly to protest against power cuts at colleges during examination periods. They went out shouting, 'We want light!', which, of course, also had another meaning. The police charged and beat them up ruthlessly, and some of the organizers were hauled off to gaol, which was a grave mistake. What the police forgot was that the students of 1967 were the children of workers, because the children of the bourgeois classes had been banned from higher education. There was a close liaison between the protesting students and factory councils, that is, between sons and fathers, and the workers could force the release of those arrested and awaiting trial.

A wave of discontent swept the country. Prices rocketed, goods became even scarcer, and the construction of much needed housing was almost at a standstill. The Novotny régime began to feel the pinch.

In December, the Central Committee of the Communist Party was summoned to an Extraordinary Session at which Novotny foolishly tried to save his skin by asking for a vote of confidence —which he did not get. The meeting had to be adjourned.

Then, like a bombshell, came the flight of Novotny's trusted military aide, Deputy Minister of Defence, General Jan Sejna, who was also Chief Liaison Officer with the Warsaw Pact forces. He sought refuge, of all places, in the United States, where it soon became known that he had tried to mobilize an armoured division in support of Novotny. To cover up the débâcle, Sejna was accused of embezzlement of funds and crooked deals involv-

[1] Dr Pfaff was finally released when the Prague Spring began. He left the country and is now a university lecturer in Switzerland.

" Before we push you over, will you kindly sign this document saying you jumped of your own free will"

8. Cummings' cartoon from the *Daily Express* at the time of Dubcek's downfall.

HIS MASTER'S VOICE

9. A British cartoonist's view of the power wielded by Trade Union leaders.

10. A gun emplacement at the holiday camp at Byala on the Black Sea which had been converted into a clubhouse.

11. Josef Frolik (centre) with his son at Byala two days before his defection.

12. Josef Frolik, London, 1974.

ing seed grain. No one in those days understood why Sejna, an arch-Bolshevik, did not go to Russia rather than the USA. The explanation was simple: the CSSR has an extradition treaty with the USSR, and it would have been difficult, even for the Kremlin, to refuse to hand him over. The Russians would rather have killed him, so Sejna wisely chose the United States as a safer refuge, with dire consequences for many Warsaw Pact secrets. Brezhnev himself rushed off to Prague but he found that little could be done to rescue Novotny's clique.

In January, 1968, the Central Committee met again and Novotny was forced to resign as the Party's General Secretary. In April he was stripped of his Presidency, and put on suspension from all functions and from the Party's membership too.

His place was taken by a comparatively little known 'compromise candidate', the somewhat shy General Secretary of the Slovak Communist Party, Alexander Dubcek, who had a good wartime record with the Partisans and, above all, a three-year course at the Party's High School in Moscow, which, in fact, became a double-edged weapon in his hands. His family background was fascinating. At one time his parents had emigrated to America, returned disappointed, and went to the Soviet Union to help to organize co-operative movements in the Ural region, where young Dubcek learnt perfect Russian. But even from there they returned disillusioned and Dubcek's father is on record as having said, 'We went to help them and they shot most of us.'

Although to begin with, I did not have much confidence in these changes and felt something along the lines of 'The King is dead, long live the King', I soon changed my mind. Sweeping reforms were introduced, and the spirit of the Prague Spring could no longer be repressed. In a way, Dubcek was carried along on the crest of a wave he could no longer control. Press censorship was abandoned and the whole truth about the Stalinist past saw the light of day in print for the first time since the communist takeover. And ugly truth it was too, especially as it was being published straight, without any beating about the bush.

The television cameras went to the people, holding interviews, especially among former political prisoners. Politicians themselves were showered with questions which would have been unthinkable only a few months earlier. When Western newspapers reappeared on the news-stands in Prague and even in the provincial capitals, people were no longer afraid to show their abhorrence of the communist past. They began to gain confidence in the new men around Dubcek, especially Leader of the Assembly, Josef Smrkovsky, Prime Minister Cernik, National Front leader Dr Kriegel, and the younger generation of politicians, such as student leader Cisar, Hajek, former Ambassador in London, now Foreign Minister, the economist Professor Ota Sik and others.

Then signs began to appear which caused the Russians and some of the satellite leaders to fear that Czechoslovakia might go the way of Yugoslavia and renounce its membership of the Warsaw Pact. Titoism became the writing on the wall for the Soviet overlords. The hated East German leader Ulbricht began to press the Russians for some action against the Czechs and their new leaders, fearing that the 'disease' might spread to his own domain, where his rule had been saved some fifteen years earlier by the Soviet tanks which crushed the workers' rebellion in Berlin. In the same way, Gomulka in Poland, Kadar (to a lesser extent) in Hungary, and, of all people, Secretary of the Ukrainian Party, Shelest, became extremely agitated by what was going on in Prague and urged Brezhnev to intervene.

In the light of all these developments, some of which were unknown to the wider public, I dropped the idea of defecting in the belief that the new era would survive all these outside pressures. Then came a visitor: it was none other than the half-forgotten Mr Choura. But now it was a different Mr Choura from the soft fat queer I had known in the last two years. The new Choura was, in fact, the harbinger of terror soon to descend yet again on my country.

SIX

Mr Choura's Revelations

When Mr Choura reappeared in July, 1968, he had transformed himself into a hard, domineering bully who treated me as if I were the agent and he were the 'case officer' running me. His sudden change of attitude was very puzzling. But a lot of things were puzzling me that July, as they were many millions of other Czechs.

It seemed as if the clock had been turned back to 1939. We were being threatened and reviled on all sides east of the Iron Curtain. Using the old techniques we had been subjected to before and after Munich, Russian, East German and Polish newspapers and radio programmes expressed their disgust at our apparent tolerance of what they cared to call 'capitalism'. The East German official mouthpiece *Neues Deutschland* (incidentally and ironically enough founded by the American CSS, the forerunner of the CIA) ran an absurd story about American troops and tanks being present in Czechoslovakia and showed photographs to prove their charge. In fact, the photographs depicted Czech soldiers and Czech tanks and half-tracks, dressed up or altered to make them look American for the shooting of the movie *The Bridge at Remagen*.

A cache of arms was reported discovered in some remote forest and trumpeted abroad as further proof that an illegal Czech organization was about to seize power, aided by the intellectuals who had just signed the Two Thousand Word Manifesto.[1] In reality the 'cache of arms' turned out to be a couple of dozen Second World War sub-machine guns planted by the Russians.

At our first meeting at the Folk House restaurant in Kladno,

[1] The Manifesto set out the responsibility of the Communist Party for the failures and crimes of the Novotny régime. It captured the spirit of the movement and of the time.

Choura seemed to indicate the way the wind was beginning to blow. After handing me a great accumulation of material, which apparently he had been hoarding for months, he returned to the subject of his interrogation by his CIA case officers in the safe house in West Berlin. First of all he said that the Americans had tried to make out that he was a KGB agent. This he had strongly denied. I nodded and wondered what he was getting at.

As the evening wore on, he launched into a tirade against the Czech Intelligence Service, saying that the CIA had penetrated it and that it was 'riddled with their agents'. 'In fact,' he cried, 'just before I left my case officer, he showed me a memo. And do you know what was on it?'

'No, what?'

'A full transcript of my last talk with you, Florian.'

'Do you mean to say that the CIA had the details on paper?'

'Yes. I do!'

'All right then, give me the text, as far as you can remember it.'

But Choura refused. He couldn't remember. All he knew was that the CIA had the details. Then he started to threaten me. He would break off his contact with me because he didn't have a safety guarantee from my service. Look what had happened to him in Berlin! He had nearly been trapped there by his American masters.

But he did not limit himself to the Czech Intelligence Service. He continued his tirade, now directing it at the new leadership of the country. Everybody knew, he said that the new leaders were in the pay of the imperialists. It was their aim to overthrow communism in Czechoslovakia and hand the country over to the Western capitalists.

For a while I was too dumbfounded to interrupt. Finally, I had had enough. 'Listen,' I said to him firmly, 'don't you realize that I could have you arrested on the spot?'

'What?' he gulped.

'You heard me,' I said. 'We have on record your own confession that you are a paid agent of the American CIA. In fact, we've got it in your own handwriting—and the fact that you have helped our service a couple of times doesn't mitigate that one little bit. Besides,' I added, 'we know that you have tried to corrupt our businessmen and officials at the Ministry of Foreign Trade with bribes in order to obtain business for yourself. Never fear, we've got a full list of your activities in that particular field too.'

That shut him up. He was terrified and started blaming the wine for his loose tongue. All the same, before we parted he again attacked the Dubcek régime, a fact which confirmed my suspicion that Choura was not only working for us and for the Americans, but also for the KGB.

My suspicion was to be confirmed two weeks later. Both of us left on seven days' vacation, Choura to spend it on the Danish coast with his boyfriend, I to Bulgaria with my family. I don't know whether Choura enjoyed his seven days of love, but I do know that we did not enjoy our stay in Bulgaria one bit. The anti-Czech mood whipped up by the Bulgarian press was so tremendous that it turned out to be a fiasco. The shopkeepers called us 'Czech swine', and we were constantly being harassed by the police, who stopped us everywhere they could and examined our papers at interminable length. Finally we gave up in despair and drove to Yugoslavia where the reception was totally different and completely friendly.

On 19 August I turned up at the Prague Institute of Micro-molecular Chemistry where I had arranged to meet Choura. But no Indian appeared. Instead, I had a different kind of visitor, a highly inefficient surveillance team. I spotted them immediately and guessed what their object was. They wanted to follow me home to find out my address—Choura knew me only by my cover name and we had always met on 'neutral' ground as it were, never in my office or home. I decided that I wouldn't give them that pleasure.

I began to dodge in and out of the narrow streets in the Dejvice area of Prague and I could soon see that my shadowers did not know the capital. A good surveillance team must know their streets by heart, every detour, every one way street, and where to arrive ahead of their suspect so that they join up with him again in a seemingly innocent and chance manner. These people were obviously strangers.

Imagine my surprise, therefore, having successfully thrown off my pursuers, to find them waiting for me at the alternative meeting place Choura and I had chosen in case he didn't turn up at the

Institute. Again no Indian, but plenty of shadowers. When I finally threw them off for a second time, I went into a little pub and had a beer to steady my nerves. It was obvious that Choura had put the tail on me and it was equally obvious where that tail had come from—*the KGB*.

I met Choura for the last time on 20 August. He turned up without any hint of an apology for his absence the previous day. Instead he behaved completely as if he were my master—which, in a way, he would be in a few hours' time, but I didn't know that then.

Once again he launched into a tirade against the rottenness of the Czech state and its leaders. Czech Intelligence had betrayed its mission by not having 'defended the interests of socialism' and it had let itself be taken over by the 'Yankee CIA'. Finally he came out with it. 'Florian,' he asked pointblank, 'how many of your people are for Dubcek, the traitor?'

Then I lost my temper completely. 'Listen, you rat,' I shouted at him, 'remember you're a mere agent and I'm your case officer! I give the orders and I ask the questions. Or,' I added, 'do you have another case officer beside myself and the Americans?'

Choura shut up like a clam. All that I could get out of him before we parted for the last time was, 'I should be glad if you would be so kind as to repeat that accusation to me tomorrow morning at six!'

Then, without any explanation as to the meaning of this enigmatic remark, my portly, black, homosexual agent was gone—for good.

I spent the next two hours discussing Choura's attitude and his curious parting remark with my chief, Major Jaroslav Borsky. For two hours we walked the empty streets together under a starlit August sky, going over that conversation time and time again and trying to discover the significance of the six o'clock meeting. What did Choura mean? Why had he picked that time of the morning? He was certainly no early riser.

Finally at about eleven o'clock we shook hands and parted company. Wearily I drove home. It had been a long, long day. Flopping into bed, I was fast asleep within minutes.

And while I slept, the first Russian paratroopers were already beginning to occupy Prague Airport, while on all our borders with the Warsaw Pact countries, 'allied' tanks were crashing through the customs posts and mowing down any Czech customs men who tried to stop them.

When I woke up the next morning, the country was occupied by the Russians. Twenty-four hours later, I was arrested.

The Defection

'Your visitation shall receive such thanks
As fits a King's remembrance.'
Hamlet, II, ii, 25

ONE

General Pavel

In the spring of 1968, the old Minister of the Interior, a close associate of the Novotny clique, was sacked. In his place Dubcek appointed General Josef Pavel, who knew the old system well and hated it; for he had suffered himself at its hands.

A pre-war communist, who had commanded a unit of volunteers in the Civil War in Spain in the late 'thirties, he had been appointed head of the People's Militia and Deputy Minister of the Interior when the communists first took over Czechoslovakia in February, 1948. He held that post until the early 'fifties when he was arrested because of his service in the Civil War—the then leader of Czechoslovakia, Klement Gottwald, claimed he had been an agent of the 'imperialists' in Spain—and he was transported to one of the very concentration camps which he had helped to found.

But Pavel was a very brave man, in spite of his past crimes against the Czech people. To make him confess to being an 'imperialist' he was tortured under the Novotny régime. But he did not break down. Within State Security he was described as a corner-stone out of which nothing could be beaten. Finally the torturers gave in; they couldn't get him to confess.

This was the man who was now appointed my chief. But Pavel was long past his best. He was a prematurely aged, kindly old man, who liked to give interviews to journalists, liked the quiet life, and talked with regret of the rose garden and cottage which he had been obliged to leave to take up his new post.

One of the first mistakes he made was to appoint Colonel Hosek as the chief of his secretariat: a man who some think had a hand in the murder of Jan Masaryk, and who had actually been involved in bringing the General himself to trial in the early 'fifties. Not exactly a person to inspire confidence in the new boss, it was thought among Intelligence personnel!

Pavel forbade the use of audio-surveillance in suspected apartments, censorship of correspondence, telephone-tapping and a whole range of other operational techniques used by every Intelligence Service throughout the world. Ordinarily this order would not have been regarded as startling, save that these surveillance techniques were not allowed even against those who were actively plotting against the new Dubcek régime. It was a very unfortunate decision. For Czech Intelligence already knew that our former Russian advisers from the KGB and their bought men in our own service were regularly meeting at a safe house in Jevany near Prague to plot the invasion of our country. Everywhere a happy Czech people were saying, 'At last we've got a Minister of the Interior of whom no one needs to be afraid!' And that was just the trouble. Nobody, including our enemies, was afraid of the old man. Thus we started to head towards our national date with destiny with an incompetent Minister in charge and a non-functioning Intelligence Service; for, as a colleague of mine remarked sadly to me one day, 'For twenty years we've been watching the West believing that any danger would come from that direction. Now it turns out to be coming from the East— *and we're completely without information!'*

But in spite of Pavel and our confused service, we were picking up odds and ends of information. Our top agent in the Headquarters of French Intelligence, code-name Samo (he's still there incidentally), passed on a report he had received from one of his men within the French Communist Party. According to him, Waldeck Rochet, head of the French CP, had obtained the approval of his own Central Committee to warn Brezhnev during a visit to Moscow not to take military action against the Czechs. In other words, some action was being considered.

A little while later, in May, our Washington Resident sent us the details of the common talk in the American capital that an Eastern bloc military attack on Czechoslovakia was expected at any time. I actually saw the telegram from the Resident through the good offices of another official who will have to remain nameless. It stated clearly that *President Johnson had been informed by the Russians that they would probably have to intervene and that they had given him assurances they would not touch American interests in Europe!*

On 24 May, the West German official spokesman, Günther

Diehl, let the cat out of the bag and revealed that there was a difference of opinion between the Germans and the Americans on how the impending crisis should be handled, when he stated, 'The Bonn Cabinet has received reliable reports that ten to twelve thousand non-Czech troops of Warsaw Pact countries will shortly enter and be stationed inside Czechoslovakia.'

As soon as the American protests started to come pouring in, Bonn denied the statement and reprimanded Diehl for 'irresponsible and panic-making talk'![1]

Naturally, what little information we could gain was passed on to Dubcek. Before he went to his celebrated meeting with the Russians at Cerna, near Cop on the Soviet border, we told him about the Johnson report. Realizing how desperate his position was, abandoned to his fate by the whole world, Dubcek blurted out to Brezhnev that if the East marched into Czechoslovakia he, in his turn, would order the Czech Army to attack West Germany in order to involve Russia in a war with NATO!

Calmly Brezhnev replied that he didn't care. Russia was prepared to risk a third world war in order to retain Czechoslovakia in its sphere of influence![2]

But in spite of the scraps of information we had garnered from the outside world most of us were caught off guard when the invasion took place. I, for instance, a senior Intelligence Officer, found out when a neighbour burst into my apartment, crying, 'The Russians are here!'

Stupidly enough, I reported to the office for duty, dodging past the great Russian tanks which I had last seen twenty or more years before at the 'dawn of the new age', and tamely allowed myself to be arrested by the new occupiers. For twenty-four hours I and the rest of my colleagues were locked up inside the building, making do with whatever food and drink we could scrounge. I was released without any form of interrogation, only to be arrested again a few days later. This time I was placed in a

---

[1] It could well be that General Gehlen's *Bundesnachrichtendienst* was behind the 'leak', for the BND seems to have been one of the first of the Western intelligence services to get the news of the forthcoming invasion. But America was too heavily involved in Vietnam to let herself be forced into an anti-Russian stance over Czechoslovakia by General Gehlen.

[2] A year later this statement was used against Dubcek with great effect when his enemies in Czechoslovakia pointed out that he was a warmonger, prepared to plunge the whole world into war to save his own neck.

deserted monastery and cross-questioned, but not very effectively. At least my interrogators did not seem to notice the burning hatred of all things Russian which now shone from my eyes. Again I was released.

But there were naturally some who were only too eager to lick the Russians' boots, who themselves were already raping Czech women and breaking into stores, as if this were 1945 and not 1968.[1] On my first day back in the office a meeting was called of all officers to discuss the situation occasioned by the invasion. At it one of the Russians' toadies proclaimed grandly, 'It is well known that there are those among us who have lost the confidence of the KGB. I have been informed by my comrades there,' he emphasized the word 'comrades' as if he had a very special claim to it, 'that they will no longer co-operate with us until those people have been removed from the Department.'

To hear such words coming from a Czech on such a day made me see red. At that moment I didn't care what happened to me. 'I would be happy for the rest of my life,' I blurted out, 'if I never saw another KGB man! Who wants their damn co-operation anyway?'

There was a murmur of approval from my colleagues.

The department head flushed violently. 'You can't talk like that, Frolik,' he snapped, 'I'll be forced to dismiss you from the Service.'

I shrugged angrily. 'What can you do? You have no power to dismiss me, anyway. You'll get me out of this service only when you and your Russian pals have fitted me out for a wooden suit.' Thereupon the meeting broke up in disorder.

Back in our office some of my like-minded colleagues said, 'Josef, you'd better get out now while the going's good.'

I shook my head. 'I'm not going—and they can't force me out. I'm staying. We've still got a job to do.'

And we had too, in spite of the occupation, or rather because of it. As the service began to split into two factions—those who supported the Russians and others like myself who still hoped that Dubcek might win—I and my friends decided we must do something active to help our hard-pressed leader.

[1] Some of the young Russian soldiers I talked to really did not know they were in Czechoslovakia. They honestly believed they were in West Germany and behaved accordingly.

For a start we set out to stop any provocative moves by the people which might cause reprisals on the part of the Soviets and an immediate take-over of the Government. Even when the KGB tried to provoke incidents, such as stone-throwing and the attempted murder of their own Ambassador to Prague, we managed to maintain control.

Then we tried to neutralize all Russian agents, whether they were within our service or working independently. Now it was their turn to come under surveillance. We followed them everywhere, using our superior knowledge of Prague's streets to keep them covered. The fact that most of the KGB men were now wearing uniform instead of civilian clothes made our task easier. But it was heart-breaking to see the number of communists of all professions and types who were now prepared to betray their homeland to the Russian bosses for a handful of silver or the promise of a job in the civil service once the 'Dubcek gang' had been kicked out.

We did not confine ourselves to espionage within our own country, although our normal contacts with the East had naturally been cut off; our borders were virtually sealed by the Warsaw Pact troops and we had no illegal network in the countries of our ex-allies. Nevertheless, we pumped foreign students returning from Moscow and Warsaw and sent others to those capitals to spy for us. We made contact with the Red Chinese who were only too glad to hurt the Soviet big brother by giving us information. We befriended Yugoslavs in Prague and got their version of what was happening. In this manner we managed to form a reasonable picture of what was going on east of our frontier and passed the information on to the Government. Thus we fought a strange secret battle with an enemy who was everywhere within our own ranks.

But I and most of my colleagues knew that we couldn't keep up the struggle much longer. Either we would be denounced to the KGB by the collaborators among us or some massive provocation in the streets would give the Russians an excuse to round up the Dubcek Government and put its members behind bars.

The danger was brought home to me strongly by a chance meeting with an old colleague, Major Jiri Francan, whom I came across in a big Prague store. 'How are you getting on, Jiri?' I asked.

151

'Collaborating like a house on fire,' came his unashamed answer, a cynical smile on his lips. 'But don't worry, Josef. Everything'll be okay soon. All we need now is a small provocation.'

'What do you mean?'

'Just any old thing which will provoke the Soviets to issue Dubcek an ultimatum—either you resign voluntarily or we move in. But this time for good! Get me?'

I got him all right. 'What kind of small provocation have you got in mind, Jiri?'

'Nothing big. Just the bombing of a Soviet command post or the vandalizing of the Soviet Book Shop or the Aeroflot offices. Then you'll see how things will fall into place. But keep it to yourself,' he leaned forward confidentially and whispered in my ear. 'Bohous Molnar is already working on a scheme.' He winked and touched the side of his big nose. 'Remember mum's the word!'

That was the first hint that our own service—or at least certain members of it, who had become traitors and Soviet lackeys—was also preparing 'provocations' which would result in Dubcek being unseated. Now we were not only fighting the Russians, we were also going to have to tackle *agents provocateurs* in our own service.

Then I knew that the end was not far off. Soon I would have to make that overwhelming decision before it was too late. Should I bolt or should I give up my resistance to the Russians and toe the line in order to save my life?

TWO

The Decision

The autumn of 1968 came and the long-range forecast said it was going to be a long, cold winter. Now more and more barrel-chested, bemedalled Soviet marshals, stinking of cheap cologne, their faces painted in the Russian fashion,[1] were arriving in Prague to threaten the Dubcek régime. In our service not a day went by without some sort of an alert or other. Even in Intelligence now we were issued with clubs, tear gas bombs, handcuffs and all the other trappings of a para-military force, as if any day a large-scale revolution might break out in the city.

Then suddenly, when the semi-finals for the world ice-hockey championship were being held in Stockholm, all this immense security apparatus was withdrawn from the streets of Prague, almost as if the authorities wanted trouble to occur; one of the participants in the semi-finals was the Russians!

As expected, the riots occurred, organized by the Major Francan had told me about—Major Motejlek, alias Molnar. Almost immediately thereafter the offices of Aeroflot were stoned and smashed by the mob, just as Francan had predicted. Again most of the security forces were conveniently absent from the scene, save one unfortunate who turned in a report that the first Czech to throw a stone was one, Vilem Novy, a member of the pro-Soviet clique. He was immediately given a severe reprimand and told, 'Don't bring in any more reports like this! Some damn progressive might get hold of the information and lay the blame for this dreadful agitation in the wrong quarter!' The *right* quarter was my opinion when I heard of the reprimand to the agent, but I kept that opinion to myself; it was now getting

[1] At one time the Czech Army was ordered to adopt the age-old customs of the Russians and use perfume and make-up. Czech officers resisted the order firmly.

F

decidedly dangerous to betray any hint of opposition to our Soviet allies.

But some were still prepared to make a stand. When our treacherous general staff officers, such as Generals Dzur, Rusov and Dvorak, together with a very drunken Soviet Marshal Grechko, appeared in Dubcek's office after the 'ice-hockey riots' to protest, he stood up to them and their threat of a military *coup d'état* if something weren't done soon to re-establish 'order'.

Going to the new President, General Svoboda, they proposed that the Soviet Army should be given the right to shoot at gatherings of more than five civilians if the Red Army soldiers thought the citizens 'lacked sufficient understanding of the strengthening of friendship with the occupiers'.

Even that arch-traitor Svoboda[1] was so horrified by this proposal that he had the drunken Russian thrown out of his office and then turned on his fellow generals and gave them a few home truths. And that was the end of that—temporarily.

All the time, young recruits and junior officers were busy conducting a private campaign of passive resistance and sabotage against the Russians. In November, 1968, for example, it was decided to refurbish a large building in Prague for use by Soviet troops and the Czech Army was given the job. In the spring of 1969 the building was turned over to the Soviets, who found to their dismay that the Czechs had played a nasty trick on them. All the lavatory and water fittings ended in the wall. The central heating came to a halt in the same place, while many of the rooms the Soviets had been expecting to use were sealed off with fake walls so that they had to search long and hard for the 'missing rooms'.

But it was obvious to us in Intelligence that it was only a matter of time before Dubcek would have to give in to the Soviets or go— the Czech David couldn't stand up to the Soviet Goliath much longer. In our Ministry Pavel had gone, to be replaced by Josef Groesser, a pro-Soviet fanatic who was actively directing Motejlek in the provocations designed to unseat Dubcek. The whole Intelligence *apparat* was now being subjected to the dictates of big brother in the East.

Many top agents of our service were now actively directed by

[1] In spite of his benign appearance he was a Soviet frontman and agent of the KGB.

the KGB and their reports retained exclusively for Russian use. Thus our agent in the British printers' union disappeared from our files one night. It was obvious where his records had gone—to Moscow.

Some of my comrades refused to take this lying down. In London, Major Frantisek Dedek wrote, for example, that this would be the last letter he would send to Prague because he was not prepared to spy any more for the *Nefachcenky*[1] at Intelligence HQ. And that was the last we heard from him.

Many undercover agents abroad, where they had—ironically enough—the freedom to do so, began to 'surface' or go over to the opposition. Others simply disappeared for good. Now we were kept busy day after day, writing up reports for the Minister on what these agents might have known of other operations and other agents.

Then suddenly two of my senior colleagues disappeared, first Captain Marous, alias Mazourek, and, a couple of weeks later, Major Ladislav Bittman, alias Brychta. There was consternation at Intelligence HQ. That very morning we were ordered to stop all activities in any area of operations that the two might have known about. Immediately we were all handed out a five-page form in which we had to enter the precise details of any operation which we might have conducted jointly with the missing men.

The days passed, until one morning, about a week or so after they had disappeared, a Major Dolezal dropped into my office. He wanted to enquire about one of our agents in the Lebanon, who seemed to be having suspicious contacts with the CIA in that country. I made him a coffee, gave him a cigarette and we started chatting about general matters. Gradually I led him round to the subject of the two missing men; in his job he would be one of the first to know what had happened to them. Dolezal, bribed by the cigarette and the coffee, let me into a secret. The 'Chief' (Minister Pelnar) already knew where the two were.

'Where?' I inquired with feigned innocence.

'In the goddam United States—that's where!' the Major exclaimed bitterly. 'The bastards have defected to the CIA!'

I tried to hide my growing excitement. 'How do you know?'

'Because our people over there have spotted them. They're being lodged in a villa in Washington, under heavy guard.

[1] An opprobrious expression for the 'Soviet advisers'.

Everywhere they go, they're surrounded by agents and guards.' Dolezal's face twisted into an ugly grin. 'But don't worry, we'll get the bastards.'

'How do you mean?' I asked. I knew now that every detail of the Czech *apparat* in Washington might one day be highly useful to me.

'We have an agent there—a Cuban émigré. Naturally he is a member of Cuban Intelligence, with which we've got a deal going.'

'A deal?'

'Yes the man in question is a trained pilot. The first opportunity he gets to smuggle himself aboard a plane being used by Bittman, he's going to hijack the plane and take it to Cuba. Then Bittman will drop into our hands like a ripe pear.'

A colleague of mine, Captain Cermak, listening to the conversation, butted in to say, 'What's the use of kidnapping the bastard now? He's probably sung to the CIA like a canary by now. Why don't we simply have his neck wrung in Washington.' He grinned. 'Give me the job. I'd gladly kill the swine. It wouldn't hurt my conscience one bit.'

Dolezal shook his head. 'No, there'll be enough time for that later. First of all we'll want him in Ruzyn (State Security prison). After we've talked with him,' he winked at me, as if I knew well what he meant by 'talking', 'then we'll kill him—*slowly*. And you know what we'll do, we'll have the killing filmed—in colour.' He grinned. 'We'll have the film shown in all departments, and after that, would-be traitors will lose all their appetite for defection.' He looked at me. 'What do you say, Josef?'

I nodded, trying to hide the trembling of my hands. 'Yes, you're right. That would be the end of any thought of defection in our department.'

But that wasn't the end of the Bittman affair. On the morning of 9 October, 1968, Major Jaroslav Borkovec burst out of his boss's office and ran down the corridor crying at the top of his voice, 'Those whores, those rotten whores!'

Alarmed by the row, I ran out of my own office and said to the crimson-faced Major, his eyes full of tears, 'What's the matter? What's up, Borkovec?'

'Are you blind?' he shouted. 'Don't you read reports? Wendland (Deputy Head of the *Bundesnachrichtendienst*) has committed suicide—and he's not the only one. There are others.'

156

'Sure, I read it; but what's it got to do with us?'

'Don't you know, *Wendland is one of our agents*!'

I must admit that statement really shook me. General Wendland, the Deputy Head of one of the West's most powerful intelligence services, a Czech agent! That really was something.[1]

Wendland, who at the age of 33 had become the youngest ever chief of the *Wehrmacht*'s Operations Department, was not the only mysterious suicide in West Germany that October. The day before he killed himself, a friend of his attached to NATO, Rear-Admiral Luedke, was found shot beside his white Taunus in the Eifel area. The village doctor who examined him proclaimed the death to be suicide. Later Bonn tried to make out it was a hunting accident, although Luedke was apparently under suspicion of espionage by MAD (German Military Intelligence).

According to MAD he had left a roll of film in a store to be developed which not only included personal photos but shots of secret NATO plans. MAD was informed. The Admiral was interrogated and then allowed to go off hunting for a few days on his word of honour as 'an officer and gentleman'.

Thus MAD's story! The reality was different. Luedke, who was chief of NATO's logistics, had a 'cosmic clearance' and knew the location of some 16,000 tactical nuclear weapons. Bittman, who ran him, had betrayed him to the CIA. In order to avoid a major scandal at a time when the German Intelligence Service, BND in particular, was coming in for some severe criticism, Luedke was allowed to take the 'gentleman's way out' by shooting himself.

Wendland's suicide followed a day later and then a whole host of them. On 14 October, another friend of the late General's, Hans Schenk, a high official in the Ministry of Economics, hanged himself in Cologne. The story was given out that he had just got married and was worried about his performance in bed!

Four days later Colonel Johann Grimm, another Wendland crony, and head of the Alarm and Mobilization Department of the Bonn Ministry of Defence, shot himself in his office. On 21 October, another official of the same Ministry was fished out of the Rhine between Cologne and Bonn. Another suicide! Bonn's comment was terse and tight-lipped. All these suicides had 'nothing to do with security matters'.

[1] At that time Wendland was even being considered as General Gehlen's successor!

Thus what is called 'Red October' in German Intelligence circles came to an end. But not quite for me. The news of Bittman's successful defection made me realize that a determined man *could* pull off a defection, if he planned it properly. It had also shown me that one couldn't 'go west' empty-handed, if one wanted to secure any protection against potential killers. One had to take information. Besides, in my mood of bitterness and disgust with my service and the way that most of my colleagues had given in to the Russians so supinely, it would give me the greatest pleasure to injure them in any way I could. That October I started to plan!

THREE

Paving the Way

My first objective was to obtain as much information as I could from the central archive of the Czech Intelligence Service, where the extremely comprehensive records went right back to the 'twenties and the start of an independent Czech Intelligence group. Naturally, I was no stranger there, and the years I had spent visiting the place paid off. Under the excuse of checking up on Choura, I managed to get myself into the section where the records of *all* present Czech agents in the West were recorded. Any Western Intelligence agent would have given his right arm for the records kept there. There was everything—the agent's real name, his detailed biography, his reports, his weaknesses, his strengths. Agents in Africa, agents in North and South America, agents by the score in every conceivable European country. As one exuberant CIA man exclaimed to me much later when he saw what I had brought with me as 'a gift': 'Joe, this goddam little lot is worth a million dollars to us!' I suppose it was.

Hour after hour, day after day, week after week, as that terrible winter of 1968 passed with one piece of bad news after another, I committed the details of these agents to memory. Hurrying home at the end of the day, my head buzzing and my eyes aching, I would lock myself into my room so that my wife and son couldn't see what I was doing (so far I had not informed my wife of my great plan) and wrote down the details I had committed to memory, using a simple code I had invented myself, with Hašek's *Good Soldier* as my key.

But I was not only interested in finding out the details of Czech agents in the archives. I wanted to know about American agents operating east of the Iron Curtain. Naturally, for my purpose, it was no use trying to discover who their 'illegals' were; they would be of no assistance. I wanted to find out who their CIA men were, attached to some embassy or consulate in some sort of legal function or other. Carefully, exceedingly carefully, I went through our detailed records, built up over the years by our counter-intelligence and surveillance teams. Some of the Americans I rejected out of hand. They were too careless, too young, too inexperienced. Others who were more experienced, I turned down because their records showed them to be under constant supervision. At last I found the man I sought right there in Prague—experienced and a known quantity (at least to our people), yet a man who was maintaining what is known in CIA circles as a 'low profile'. 'Mr Low Profile' was my man! For obvious reasons, I must keep this contact intentionally vague.

I contacted him simply enough. Although I may not say how I did it, it was far easier than I had imagined. In spite of what is said about the CIA's love of secrecy, I am sure there is no other intelligence service in the world whose HQ is signposted as 'CIA Turn Off', which is the case on US Highway Number One between Washington and Foster Dulles Airport.

A few days later I deliberately ran my little Skoda into a wall. When they heard, my few remaining friends in Intelligence pulled my leg, saying that I was letting things get on my nerves, or was it because I had just been awarded the Order of Merit by the President on account of my work with Bakalar and Igl. I smiled wanly and let them have their joke. My damaged mudguard was vital for the next stage of my defection.

I met Mr Low Profile at the garage to which I took my car for repairs, just as we had planned. There, in the little suburban garage which was the CIA's safe house, we could talk at length and in complete safety.

The agent was exactly as I had imagined him to be, neither too young nor too old, too cautious nor too bold. And he did not hesitate to tell me the truth, although I knew that his fingers must have been itching to get hold of me then and there. (I must have been far the greatest prize that had ever come his way.) As he saw it, the CIA could not be involved in any provocative act in Czechoslovakia. The situation was too serious. 'There is only one way out for you, Mr Frolik. (I had told him my real name to show my trust in him.) You can't go west—the border is too heavily guarded. Yugoslavia is out of the question too. The border eastwards is pretty easy though.'

'Yes, to Siberia,' I quipped.

'How right. But this is what I suggest. You people still have links with Bulgaria, though God knows how long they will last. Now, Mr Frolik, if you can get to Bulgaria, our people can get you out.'

'How? From within Bulgaria?'

'No. From Turkey across the Black Sea. Once you're that far, with a bit of luck, we can get you out without any trouble.'

'All right then, Bulgaria it is,' I said slowly, though I had no idea of how I was going to do it.

Before we parted, Mr Low Profile took my hand firmly in his and pressed it hard. 'Get to the Black Sea, Mr Frolik, and I promise you on my word of honour, you'll be in Washington within three days.'

After nearly two decades of Intelligence I had little faith left in 'words of honour' given so easily and broken just as easily, but somehow I trusted this American. He would keep his word. But how the hell was I going to get an exit visa for Bulgaria?

Then luck played my way. A week or so after my meeting with the 'opposition', with my nerves on edge and my wife worried sick because her father had been taken to hospital with cancer, I chanced to get into conversation with one of my colleagues who asked me, 'Josef, do you know anything about our new camp at Byala?' My heart almost stopped beating. Byala is in Bulgaria!

'Why indeed!' I said. 'I know that part of Bulgaria very well. I've been there a couple of times. Why?'

'Well, I'm off for a couple of weeks' holiday soon. Apparently our people have given the Bulgars a camp for their intelligence people in the High Tatras (the mountainous region of Slovakia). In return their Ministry has given us one at Byala on the Black Sea.' He smiled. 'For select people naturally.' 'Naturally,' I smiled back, though I had never felt less like smiling in my life. An idea was beginning to dawn in my mind.

'Yes,' my colleague continued. 'Nobody here knows much about the place. I mean what kind of gear to take, or whether we can get things like Czech beer there?'

'Well, that's one thing you definitely won't get there,' I said. 'But the wine's all right.'

'You seem to know something about it,' he said. 'What about

giving us—and there's a lot of us who'd like to go, seeing we can't go to Yugoslavia this summer—a little talk on the Black Sea?'

Thus it came about that I gave a couple of short lectures, illustrated with slides I had taken in previous years, of my experiences in Bulgaria and on the Black Sea; and all the time I was watching those sun-drenched beaches on the screen, a little voice within me was saying, *'This is the way out.'*

At the beginning of June, I put in for my annual summer leave of four weeks and requested permission to spend it at the Intelligence Camp at Byala, beginning on 23 June, 1969.

It was three weeks ahead and the time had come to let my wife into my secret. One afternoon after work we drove out some thirty kilometres from Prague, the names of 400 agents already cemented into the floor of my car, unknown naturally to my wife, already so upset by her father's illness. There in the woods we walked like a courting couple, free of any bugging or surveillance. We walked for what seemed a long time. Finally I couldn't hold out any longer. I told her, in four simple words which signified the start of a completely new life for us, 'I'm going to defect.' Her face crumpled suddenly and she began to cry. I comforted her and after a while she stopped. 'But why, Josef?' she asked.

'Because I can't stop here any longer. I hate what the Russians have done to our country. I must get out!'

'But my father,' she protested. 'He's to be operated on on the nineteenth.'

'I know,' I reassured her. 'And we'll still be here to see him after he comes out. I've applied for leave on the 23rd. It's our last opportunity. You know as well as I do that my dismissal is bound to be announced by the 30th and after that the frontier is closed for me.'

'But Josef . . .' Her voice broke and she could say no more.

But on the way back she pressed my arm softly and whispered, 'All right, Josef, let's go; but promise me that I'll see Father after the operation.'

I nodded, automatically keeping my eyes on the rear mirror to check if I were being followed. 'I promise,' I said numbly and we drove the rest of the way back to Prague in silence.

Then the trouble occurred. On the fifteenth I was informed by my chief that I was going to be dismissed from the service as anti-Russian and suspect, with effect from 1 August, 1969. Privately he told me I was lucky to get away with a dismissal; there were those who were demanding my head.

I muttered my thanks and left his office in a daze. After so many years of service, I was going to be kicked out of Intelligence, the only job I had ever known. But that wasn't so important. For there was an Intelligence rule that no one could leave the country *for five years* after being dismissed the Service. If I didn't manage the trip to Bulgaria by that date, I should be stuck in Czechoslovakia for good, a victim of the ever-changing moods of the Russians and their toadies within my former department. *I had to get out by Monday, 23 June!*

If that wasn't enough trouble, the hospital where my father-in-law was to be operated on postponed the date of the operation by a day. My wife was frantic with worry and begged me to let her see the old man once more; the doctors assured her that he wouldn't have much longer to live after the operation. I promised. There was nothing else I could do, for I had not yet received the vital permission to leave from the Chief of the Intelligence Directorate to which I belonged. Now it almost looked as if my long-planned defection would have to be postponed indefinitely.

My nerves began to go. I snapped at the secretaries in the office and even at my few remaining friends in Intelligence. My little boy started to feel the strain too, although he didn't know why his father and mother were so nervous. His face grew pale, in spite of the glorious sunshine outside and more than once he woke up in the middle of the night screaming. I took to hanging around the office of the Chief of the Directorate, whose signature on my permit to leave for Bulgaria was now so vital. But I daren't go in and ask for the permit; I knew I was under suspicion and such a move might trigger off my arrest.

My father-in-law was operated on on a Friday. We visited him on Saturday and Sunday. He was in a bad way. The doctors shook their heads afterwards. 'Not much hope of him seeing the week out,' one of them told my wife. But she wouldn't give up hope. 'Josef,' she urged me more than once during that terrible weekend, 'let's stay. Accept your resignation and let's see if we can't find a job for you as an accountant. *Please*, Josef.'

Not trusting myself to speak, I shook my head numbly. There was no turning back now. I couldn't trust the Russians and their Czech lackeys. They might let me go on 1 August and arrest me before the end of the month to ship me off to God knows where. Then my wife and son would never see me again. Of that I was sure.

Monday came, the day we were supposed to leave for Bulgaria. The Skoda was already packed, the top secret documents under the floor, sleeping bags in the rear just in case we had to make a run for it and had to sleep rough. Time and again my wife looked down from the windows of our flat at the car below, as if it were an invention of the devil itself, some fiendish machine that would take us away from her father, friends and homeland for ever. And in the long run she was right.

It was now eight o'clock on the morning of 23 June. I had to take the bull by the horns. Deliberately putting on my holiday clothes, I went to the office. If I couldn't get the permit this morning, my defection would be off.

Luck was with me again. My own chief was not in. For a few minutes I was at a loss. What the devil could I do now? Then I thought of the Chief of Personnel. He was responsible indirectly for my welfare too. Couldn't he sign my leave permit?

Hurriedly, I strode down the corridor to his office, knowing that he was my last hope. I knocked and was asked to enter by a familiar voice. It was that of a pretty young secretary, who had been an enthusiastic member of the audience when I had given one of my talks on Bulgaria. 'Ah Major Frolik,' she said, 'you look very summery!'

'Of course,' I said, forcing myself to smile. 'I'm going on a month's holiday to Bulgaria.'

'Where else, for our expert on the subject?'

'But there's a problem. My chief's away and I need a signature.'

'Is that all?' Swinging her attractive legs from beneath her desk, she took a new form. 'Fill that in,' she said. I'd done it in a flash and a moment later she disappeared into the office of her chief, Podzemny.

Five minutes passed by in pure unadulterated agony. Then she returned, her face wearing a broad smile. 'Here you are Major.' Blindly I looked down at the paper. Podzemny had scribbled his initials beneath it. *I had my permit!* 'Good-bye, Major—and have a good time in Byala,' she called as I opened the door to leave her office—for the last time.

'Good-bye and thank you very much,' I replied, trying to control my voice. At that moment, I could have hugged her till I had squeezed all the breath out of her body.

FOUR

The Escape

The weather was marvellous. Day after day the sun shone white-hot and brilliant over a calm, sparkling blue sea that stretched into the distance towards Turkey and freedom, so temptingly close yet as far away from us at that moment as the moon.

But if nature was beautiful at Byala the company at Camp Praha—Czech for Prague—was decidedly ugly. It was full of collaborators from Czech Intelligence and their pals from the Bulgarian service, all of them so full of cheap Bulgarian cognac that their revolutionary feeling increased proportionally to the octane rating of their blood.

I hated them—each and every one of them. It took me all my strength of will to restrain myself from smashing my fist into their grinning, drunken faces when they started boasting to the Bulgarians of how they had helped the 'Soviet brothers' to put down the 'Czech insurrection'. But with rescue so close I contained myself.

Each morning, playing the casual, carefree holiday-maker, I and my family threaded our way through the other Czech tourists in the adjoining Luna Camping site and spent the day on the beach, waiting for the CIA man to contact me, for by now Mr Low Profile would know where I was. Hour after hour I stared at the horizon, while my son played happily on the sands, as if by doing so I could drag Turkey and freedom across to me.

Once I was forced to break my routine and attend a party given by the camp leaders for a Bulgarian Intelligence delegation, headed by a loud-mouthed Bulgarian General, with a face puffy from too much drinking and decked out in full uniform, in spite of the heat. The party took the usual course of such affairs. Much drinking, lots of loud-mouthed toasts to 'our brothers in the Soviet Union' and praise of those who had put down the 'counterrevolution in Czechoslovakia'. Finally the General stood up, swaying dangerously in his highly polished jackboots, and launched into an attack on my country; 'You, comrades, are the flower of the Czech working class,' he thundered. 'You of State Security are the only ones in Czechoslovakia who did not sell out to the capitalists and their minions in Prague. You stood firmly on the side of the Soviet Union and held high the flag of revolution.' He could hardly wait for the interpreter to keep up with him. 'The Czechoslovak Communist Party, riddled with renegades, traitors to communism and paid agents of imperialism, has committed wholesale treason.'

There was an enthusiastic roar of approval from the drunken Czech Intelligence men and I had to clench my fists to prevent myself shouting out that he was a liar.

'Yes, comrades,' the General continued. 'The time has come when the Czech Communist Party must be thoroughly purged of all such treacherous elements!'

The end of his speech was greeted by loud applause and then one of my colleagues, Major Vaclav Trousil, his froglike legs supporting a massive overhanging beer belly, struck up the *Partizan* song. Everyone joined in with enthusiasm.

But the crowd of Czechs from the nearby Luna Park who had been attracted by these antics were not as laudatory as the toadying Intelligence men. They started to make threatening gestures. Soon they were calling their fellow countrymen 'whores, traitors, rotten collaborators' and so on. The singing was brought to a premature conclusion with the *Internationale*, after which, followed by the angry cries of the Czech tourists, the 'flower of the Czech working class' fled to the safety of Camp Praha's restaurant where they could continue their drinking in peace.

On that particular day I was proud of my countrymen and happy for a while. But now after fourteen days of waiting for the contact, the strain was beginning to tell. I was beginning to feel that, if he or she did not turn up soon, I would lose my nerve and break down.

To make matters worse, three of my colleagues had attached themselves to us, Majors Trousil, Kraml and Necasek, following me everywhere I went. And I could guess why. Prague had informed the camp leaders that I was to be dismissed the Service on 1 August and they had been appointed to watch over me. They were taking no chances.

Then I caught the bug, which afflicted everyone sooner or later at Camp Praha. The heavy Bulgarian cuisine, replete with lots of yoghurt and unwashed tomatoes and peppers, wreaked havoc with the toughest stomach, even those full of the local cognac. Now when I went to the beach in the morning, I had to station myself close to the rather primitive iron-roofed beach latrines, which advertised their function by a nauseating odour, made no better by the heat waves rippling off the roof. Regularly every hour or so I felt the familiar twinge in my stomach and with a hasty excuse to my family and my colleagues I would make a quick dash for the stinking latrines, sweating both with the heat and the apprehension that I might not make it in time.

But my bug did have one small consolation. It kept my three colleagues off my back a little. The smell of the latrines and the frequency of my visits held them at bay. Instead of one of them accompanying me each time, the three of them preferred to laze in the hot sand, drinking Bulgarian beer and watching the dark-skinned charms of the local beauties in their skimpy bikinis.

It was fortunate that they did so. For it was in the latrine of all places that the CIA eventually contacted me. The contact was a typical young Bulgarian, dark-haired, hook-nosed, wearing nothing but swimming trunks and a silver identity bracelet. He sat down in the open cubicle next to me and asked: 'Mister Frolik—Mister Josef Frolik?'

'Yes,' I answered. 'How did you know my name?' He did not answer my question. Instead, keeping his eyes fixed on the entrance, he began to brief me on what I was to do.

'It's too difficult here. Your and my people are everywhere. We have decided, therefore, that you must make the next stage elsewhere. You've got to get out of Byala'.

'But how? They're suspicious as it is.'

'Tell them you're returning to Czechoslovakia. Any excuse will do for them,' he replied.

'*Czechoslovakia*,' I gasped. 'That would be fatal . . .'

He held up his hand for me to be quiet, not taking his eyes off the door for an instant. 'Of course, you won't go there. Our man will contact you—not more than twenty kilometres from here.

He'll give you further instructions. If you tell your shadows you are returning home, they won't be suspicious. All they'll do is to wire ahead that you are coming and let your people at the other end take care of the problem.'

'Yes,' I agreed. 'You're right. They won't want to interrupt their holiday.'

He nodded, as if, for him at least, the matter was settled. 'All right, Mr Frolik, you have forty-eight hours. You leave here on the evening of the fourteenth of July.'

Without even a goodbye, he rose hurriedly and disappeared as abruptly and mysteriously as he had appeared. I never saw him again.

The sudden appearance of the Bulgarian contact man cured my stomach instantly. But I didn't tell my shadows that. All the following day I kept up my periodic dashes to the latrine, making them more frequent than ever, so that the trio of majors became too bored with my departures even to bother to laugh any more. All that day I skipped meals, so that by the evening I presented a hollow-eyed, pale-faced appearance which contrasted strongly with the bronzed, healthy, happy figures all around me.

That night I took my wife for a moonlight stroll along the beach, where I was sure that no bugging device would work against the permanent rumble of the waves, and told her about the contact and my plan for the morrow.

The morning of the fourteenth dawned bright and hot. As always I took my family down to the beach and as usual we were joined a little later by my shadows. With as much casualness as I could achieve in my tense state, I remarked, 'I've had a bellyful of this place.'

'You can say that again, Josef,' Necasek said. 'But I thought it was the other end that was troubling you!'

'Yes. It's this damn food here. I mean, what can you expect on the kind of food they dish up in the camp.' I faked a groan, as if I had just experienced another twinge of pain. 'I've had it. This bug of mine won't go away, even though I starved myself all day yesterday. I think we ought to try a rather less warm climate and simpler food.'

'What do you mean, Josef?' Kraml asked, a little suspiciously.

I shrugged. 'Well, I thought we ought to go back home, get away from this food and sun.'

'But you've still got over a week of your vacation left,' Kraml said.

'I know. I might spend a couple of days at Lake Balaton (a resort area in Hungary) on my way home. It's cooler there and the Hungarian food might clear my guts up. It'll be a change from all this yoghurt stuff.'

'Yes, I agree,' my wife chimed in, as I had briefed her to do the previous evening. 'I've had enough of this sun too.' She hesitated. 'Besides I'm anxious about my father—he's very ill, you know.' Kraml nodded. At that moment I could have hugged my wife. The remark about her father had taken a lot of courage, especially as she knew now that she would never see him again.

The three shadows sank down again on the beach to sleep off their hangovers. We had fooled them. Lake Balaton was pretty big. It would be a couple of days before the Hungarian security people could wire them that a Major Josef Frolik of Czech Intelligence had not arrived; and it would be another day before they received similar information from our Border Police. Now I had three whole days without supervision in which to make my escape. I could have cried out with joy there and then. Instead I played my role to the bitter end. Excusing myself, hands clutched to my belly, I made another quick dash for the latrines.

The man stopped me just before sunset on the secondary road we had picked for our journey north. 'Bit more interesting than the main road,' I had told our shadows, carrying out their surveillance to the bitter end. 'Perhaps we can see something of the country that way.' He was bent over the bonnet of a square-set, old-fashioned looking East German Wartburg, apparently tinkering with the engine. As soon as he heard our car he turned round, spanner in hand, and waved us down. I stopped immediately. This must be our man. His greeting in my native language in the middle of the wilds of Bulgaria confirmed my assumption.

'I wonder if you could help me, comrade? I see you're Czech by your number-plate and I spent several happy years in your beautiful country.'

'What is it?' I asked.

'I don't exactly know,' he said. 'The petrol doesn't seem to be getting through to the motor.' I could see him more clearly now in the gathering gloom. He was about my age, with a strong chin and cold, unworried eyes, as if he were used to situations of this kind. He could have come from anywhere in Central Europe. Perhaps a Sudeten German, which would account for his excellent Czech. But I never did find out, though I asked about him later in Washington.

'Let me have a look,' I volunteered. 'It wouldn't be very nice to get stuck out here all night.'

'You can say that again' the CIA agent agreed as we bent our heads together under the bonnet.

'Nice to meet you, Mr Frolik. I'm glad you were able to shake off your shadows.' He tapped the cylinder block a couple of times loudly. Behind us in the Skoda, my wife watched the road anxiously. But it was completely empty. The farmers with their lumbering, ox-drawn carts had gone home and the only cars that would be out now would be those of a few unsuspecting tourists. We were safe, it seemed, from observation or interference.

'All right, Mr Frolik,' the man whispered. 'We're going to get you out tomorrow night at a spot on the Gulf of Burgas. You'll find a detailed map in the Wartburg. The Gulf is the closest we can safely get to Turkey. The closer you get the stricter Bulgarian security becomes. However, we've done it before and undoubtedly we'll do it again. You must be in position at the spot indicated by twenty-three hundred hours. Ditch the car before you get there. You will be picked up by boat at that exact spot at exactly that time.'

I nodded my understanding.

'All right then, that's about it. Now this is what I'm going to do. I shall drive up to the next bend and into the wood. You follow in five minutes and you'll find the Wartburg there with the key in the ignition and the marked map in the glove compartment.'

'And my car?'

'Just leave it there. When you've gone, I'll see that it is dealt with so that it appears that you have met with an accident.'

'All right, I understand.'

I understood only too well why the CIA did not want my defection to be discovered for as long as possible. They knew by now from Mr Low Profile that I was coming to them 'bearing gifts'. They would want all the time they could gain to evaluate those gifts without alarming the Czech authorities. With a bit of luck, the Americans reasoned, they would be able to arrest every agent whose name I could give them while they were still unwarned. It would be a great coup if they could pull it off.

To keep up the little game we were playing, just in case we were being observed, which was highly unlikely, the man got into the front seat and made a great play of trying to start the engine. Finally, it burst into life. He got out and shook my hand. 'Well, thank you very much for your kind assistance, comrade. I hope I can help you some time,' he said loudly, and then under his breath, 'Remember tomorrow night at twenty-three hundred precisely . . . and the best of luck!' With a final wave he was gone. I hung around, pretending to be cleaning my hands on a tuft of grass. Then, when the five minutes were up, I followed him round the bend and into the woods, where I could just make out the squat shape of the Wartburg in the gloom. Swiftly I transferred my wife and son into the other car before going to work on the floor of the Skoda where I had cemented in the vital list of agents' names and particulars. In the stillness of the woods the noise of my hammer breaking the cement seemed to make as much racket as a large-scale industrial plant working full out. But the noise was a risk I had to take.

Finally, I got through to the documents encased in their plastic covering. I tossed them to my wife and she stowed them in the back of the car underneath our sleeping bags, the only things (apart from one small case full of such personal items as family photos) we were taking with us. Although the mysterious contact man had not ordered us to leave anything behind, I reasoned he might be able to use our clothes etc. to fake an accident more convincingly. Then I covered the Skoda with branches so that the casual observer at least could not spot the car from the road; I had no idea how long it would be before the CIA agent's men came to deal with it. One last look around to check if everything was all right, a swift glance at the controls of the new car to familiarize myself with them and then I engaged first gear and we were off the way we had come, driving down the empty road for the Gulf and our rendezvous with the CIA men from Turkey.

It was very dark. There was no sound save the soft lap of the waves, the occasional cry of some night bird and the gentle rustle of the wind in the trees among which we had been hiding most of that long, nerve-racking day.

It had been a hellish wait. One thing our contact had forgotten was that we would need food and drink, in particular the latter. We had little of either, save for a couple of very sweet, soft Bulgarian chocolate bars and two bottles of beer, which had made up our diet for the day. We daren't leave our cover to buy food at the little villages which dotted that pleasant stretch of the coast. Our Czech language would have given us away at once. The Gulf of Burgas seemed to be visited only by Bulgarians and a handful of East Germans, whose unmistakable Wartburgs we had watched all day driving along the narrow, dusty roads near our hide-out.

Fortunately, our son, now fast asleep with my jacket as a pillow, had not found anything strange in the diet of melting chocolate and warm, fizzy beer. That had been one consolation. But now the sun had gone down and the leaden hours of waiting had almost passed. For the twentieth time I looked at my watch. Fifteen minutes to go, I told myself, firmly swearing that I would not look at my watch again, only to do so a minute later. Next to me my wife whispered anxiously, 'Do you think they're going to come, Josef?'

I pressed her arm reassuringly. 'Of course they'll come. They haven't gone to all this trouble for nothing. Besides they know as well as you do that I've got some very pretty presents for them in Washington.'

'I hope you're right.'

'Of course I'm . . .'

I never finished the sentence. The silence was broken by the faint chug-chug of a powerful engine somewhere out in the darkness. I turned my head to one side and strained hard. There was no mistaking it. There was a boat out there somewhere, running at very slow speed.

The sound of the boat was getting ever closer. 'Listen,' I whispered to my wife, 'I'm going out there. If it's a Bulgarian patrol boat, get the boy and run for it. Later you can tell the authorities you didn't know what I was up to. I simply ditched you with the car. They won't hurt you.' I didn't give her time to protest. Pushing her arm aside, I rose and doubled to the edge of the water, running awkwardly through the wet sand. Now I could make out the boat, a dark rakish shape, with a thin bone of white water in its teeth. On her deck in the faint green glow that

173

was coming from the sloping-roofed cabin, I could just recognize the figure of a man, head cocked to one side, as if he were listening intently. A voice called something in a language I couldn't understand. It wasn't a Slavic language. Of that I was sure. Was it Turkish? I called back and waved my arms. A thin white light flicked on. It swung round the water's edge until it fell on me. I threw my hands in front of my eyes, temporarily blinded. For a long moment it stayed there, illuminating me in its bright whiteness. Suddenly it went out and left me blinking in the darkness. Then a happy voice shouted, 'We've seen you Mr Frolik. One minute; we're coming to get you. Just one minute please.' The voice was reassuringly American.'

Thereafter things happened fast. Once aboard the launch, manned by Turkish smugglers and two members of the CIA, we swung out into the Black Sea at seventy kilometres an hour. Down below, sipping whisky, we could feel the boat vibrate under our feet. We were on our way to freedom. Once, just before we left Bulgarian territorial waters, the Turkish skipper, a dark-haired gigantic rogue with one eye, slowed down rapidly and there was an anxious moment when we thought we were heading on the same course as a Bulgarian patrol boat. But the ship turned out to be a little coastal freighter, heading perhaps for Varna or Constanta, and we flashed by in a great cloud of white spray, even before the lookout had time to call out.

An hour later we were in Istanbul! But we had no time for sight-seeing. After all we were in Turkey illegally and my rescuers wanted no trouble with the government of a country which leaned over backwards to allow them to carry out their mysterious midnight trips across the Black Sea. Immediately we were taken to the little US Air Force Base in the city's suburbs. My wife and son were re-clothed in what I took to be typical American garments from the PX (my son received his first pair of jeans, the plague of my life ever since), while some anonymous major in the US Air Force volunteered to sacrifice his uniform for me. Thus equipped, my family and I boarded a US Air Force plane.

The details of my journey are uninteresting to relate thereafter. All that needs to be told is that we arrived in Washington, having stopped on the way at Trieste, on 21 July, 1969, the same day that the first two earthmen, Aldrin and Armstrong, stepped out onto the soil of the moon. For me that landing in Washington was just as great an achievement!

Surrounded by CIA men and the Secret Servicemen who had been assigned to guard me, I was hustled through customs to meet no less a person than Richard Helms, the head of the CIA himself. He shook my hand and said enthusiastically, 'Joe, the telegrams are going out from Prague to your embassies and Intelligence agencies throughout the world. And do you know what they are saying?'

I shook my head, bewildered by everything which had happened to me in these last seventy-two hours.

The Director grinned happily. 'I'll tell you: *"Stop all activity. Frolik has defected".*'

Envoi

This has been the story of one man's defection—the agony, the soul-searching, the frustration of having to make that overwhelming decision to break and run, never to return.

It has brought me freedom—and danger too. For the long arm of communist retribution and vengeance can cross even oceans. In the United States, unfortunately, there are enough drug-crazed, psychopathic young men who will kill for as little as a hundred dollars. Two attempts have been made on my life in the last four years—once a severed brake system in my car and once an empty car crashing mysteriously through the window of my office. As a result, I had to move yet again, starting a new job and assuming a new identity, waiting at nights for that telephone call in Czech, which would tell me that my new cover had been broken.

Yet I can take the danger. Freedom is worth it; it is something which those of us who know and hate the communist system are prepared to pay the highest price for. I can accept the fact, too, that I have lost my world. For the rest of my life, I know and accept, I must talk and think in another language; I must eat the food of that other culture; never again see my golden Prague. In the final analysis there is no substitute for one's homeland and there can never be any escape from the memories of the past.

Was all that long agony of mind and the danger of the escape worth it then, you may ask? *One hundred per cent!* For where can the hopes and dreams of my occupied people be freely published save in the West? And who can express those hopes save those of us who enjoy the freedom the West offers?

But that has not been the only reason for my writing this account of my defection. I hope my story will serve to warn the vast majority of complacent, well-meaning and basically *honest* people in the West that the Soviets will never cease to attempt to achieve their aim of world domination. In Moscow they speak of détente and co-existence between East and West. Yet the great war in the shadows between the two major world power blocs continues day by day, week by week, year by year. Thus if the Soviets realize they cannot conquer from *without*, by military force, they will try to do so from *within*, using subversion, corruption, blackmail, bribery; and there are enough fools—and rogues—in the West always prepared to become their tools.

As I write, for instance, a delegation has arrived in the United Kingdom from the so-called 'Parliament' of my native country, headed by the quisling Jan Marko, appointed Foreign Minister in the puppet Government imposed on Czechoslovakia by the Soviets after their armed take-over. Undoubtedly, this delegation, invited by their counterparts in the 'Mother of Parliaments' at Westminster, will be wined and dined everywhere in London. After all didn't the Prime Minister, Mr Wilson, state in Prague in 1973 that the events of 1968 were 'best forgotten'? Yet those same 'fraternal delegates' from Prague enter England with subversion and corruption in their already corrupt minds. They, too, like I once, and every other official representative of the Czech State, will be on the lookout for likely candidates among those British 'parliamentary free-loaders', as Mr Bernard Levin so aptly calls them, to recruit as agents and contacts.

As the bearer of a great name in English history wrote in a letter to *The Times* on 21 November, 1974:[1] '(This) visit is no less objectionable than would have been a similar delegation from Nazi-occupied Czechoslovakia. Have the authors of this misguided invitation paused to consider the feelings of those Czechoslovak patriots who even now languish in prison and labour camps and the millions of the Czechoslovak people who yearn to be free? Those of us who look forward to the day when we can welcome to the Mother of Parliaments a Czechoslovak delegation representing the Parliament of a free people, can only express their deep regret that the British Parliament should be invited to connive at a grisly charade.'

How right Mr Winston Churchill is!

No aid whatsoever should be given to such people, who will only use it for propaganda purposes back home in order to make

[1] Winston S. Churchill, MP.

their repressive puppet government appear more legitimate; for after all, has it not been recognized by one of the West's greatest and oldest democracies!

Let us make no mistake. The cold war in which I fought—*on the wrong side*—for nearly eighteen years is aimed at one thing only—*conquering you*.

Index

Josten, Josef, 65–6, 70; plans to assassinate him, 66–9, 71
Jundi, Colonel, 127, 129

Kadar, Janos, 138
Kavan, Colonel Antonin, 121
KGB, the, xii, 2, 10, 27, 35, 46, 50, 57, 78, 80, 103, 124, 127, 128n., 129, 134, 140–2, 148, 150, 151, 154n., 155
Khrushchev, N. S., xii, 20
Kindl, Vaclav (V. Nodat), 22–3
Koska, Major Jan (Klecka), 16–17, 68, 78–81, 99–101, 103–4, 108 and n., 109, 113–14
Koutsky, Vladimir, 27, 67
Kraml, Major, 167, 169–70
Kriegel, Dr., 138
Krogers, the, KGB spies, 35, 36n.
Krokodil, 131
Kroupa, Lt.-Colonel Vlastimil, 67
Kutyepov, General, 102

Lebl, Josef, 89
'Lee', British Labour M.P., 58–9, 96–7
Leimer, Willy, 20n., 22, 23 and n., 27, 29
'Lev', *see* Hodac, Jaroslav
Levin, Bernard, 71, 98, 177
Lieskovsky, Captain Milan, 118
'Light', agent, *see* Zbytek, Charles
Literary News, 135
Litvinov, Colonel, 35–7
Lomsky, General, 126
Lonsdale, Gordon, *see* Molody
Louda, Major, 49
Luedke, Rear-Admiral, 157

MAD (German Military Intelligence), 157
Maki, Eugene, *see* Hayhanen, Reino
Malek, Bohumil, 43–6, 49, 69, 78–9
Mara, Anna, 53
'Marconi', *see* Praeger, Nicholas
Mark, Mr. and Mrs., 35, 37–8

Marko, Jan, 71, 177
Marous (Mazourek), Captain, 155
Masaryk, Jan, 70, 147
Mau-Mau movement, 118
Mauthausen concentration camp, 7, 26
Menon, Krishna, 134
MI5, 23, 36, 44, 45, 49, 66, 81, 82, 93, 100–2, 106–8
Minx, Major, 78, 85–6
Molnar, Major Bohous (Motejlek), 33–4, 60, 152–4
Molody, Kanon Timofievich (Gordon Lonsdale), 35–8
Moravec, Major Villem, 100–1
Massad (Israeli Intelligence Service), 125
Motejlek, Major, *see* Molnar
Mrazek, Major Jan ('Ptacek') ('John'), 39–41, 49–50, 56, 68, 78
Müller, SS General Heinrich, 21–2, 29

Nachtmann, Soviet double-agent, 20–1, 27, 29
Nasser, President, 131
National Union of Mineworkers, 88
NATO, 59, 60, 97, 114, 123, 157; headquarters in London, 82–5, 92
Naujocks, Alfred, 59
Nazis, the, 7, 8, 21, 26, 62
Necasek, Major Jaroslav, 167, 169
Necvalec, Major, 25, 28n.
Nemec, Dr. Jan, 64
Nemec, Major Jaroslav, 33, 34, 60
Neues Deutschland, 139
Neumann, General, 67
New, E., 133
New York Times, 136
Nicholls, Harry, 89
NKVD, the, 20n., 22, 29, 89
Novotny, President Antonin, 20, 51, 67, 68, 115, 135–7, 139n., 147; and Barak, 25–8; spy for the Gestapo, 26; downfall, 137

Sudeten Germans, 60–1
Sunday Times, 136
Svoboda, General Ludvik, 154
Svoboda-Sochor, First Lieutenant Antonin, 67
Syria, 126–31; Ba'ath Party, 127, 131; Communists, 127, 131; Russian role in, 130–1; and Red China, 130

Taborsky, Lt.-Colonel Vaclav, 35, 37, 44, 65, 66, 71, 113–14
Times, The, 66, 71n., 98, 178
Tito, Marshal, and Titoism, 131, 138
Tlas, Major-General, 130
'Topaz' ('Saphyr'), KGB agent, 124
Trade Unions in Britain, 85–92; and Communists, 87–8
Transport and General Workers' Union, 88, 89
Trhlik, Dr., Czech Ambassador in London, 78
Trotsky, Leon, 102
Trousil, Vaclav, 167
TUC, the, 88–9; Brighton Conference (1965), 89
Tuzex coupons, 94
Two Thousand Word Manifesto, 139 and n.

Ulbricht, Walter, 138
Ulik, S., 89
Urban, F., 51
Uris, Leon, 124
US Embassies: London, 106–8; Paris, 72; Prague, 120

Valek, Jan, 49
'Venus', *see* Bianchi, Gina
Vilim, Blazej, 69–70
Voda, Senior Police Lieutenant Pavel, 54–6
Vosjoli, Philippe de, 124

Waldeck Rochet, 148
War in the Shadows, The (Whiting), 30
Wendland, General, 156–7
West Germany, 14, 15, 50, 59–63, 158; Military Intelligence, 157; Ministry of Defence, 157
Whiting, Charles, 30
Wilson, Harold, and Wilson Government, 97–8, 177
Wilson, Jock, 107
World Federation of Trade Unions (WFTU), 88–9
Wynne, Greville, 36n.

Zbytek, Charles ('Light') ('Charlie Charles'), 50–3, 56, 68
Zionists, 120, 121